SNOW KISS

This Large Print Book carries the
Seal of Approval of N.A.V.H.

SNOW KISS

Amy Marie Sandrin

Thorndike Press • Waterville, Maine

Published in 2006 by arrangement with Amy Sandrin.

Thorndike Press® Large Print Romance.

The tree indicium is a trademark of Thorndike Press.

The text of this Large Print edition is unabridged.
Other aspects of the book may vary from the original edition.

Set in 16 pt. Plantin by Christina S. Huff.

Printed in the United States on permanent paper.

Library of Congress Cataloging-in-Publication Data

Sandrin, Amy, 1961–
    Snow kiss / by Amy Marie Sandrin. — Large print ed.
      p. cm. — (Thorndike Press large print Thorndike
romance)
    ISBN 0-7862-8260-6 (lg. print : hc : alk. paper)
    1. Skiing — Fiction.   2. Denver (Colo.) — Fiction.
3. Colorado — Fiction.   4. Large type books. I. Title.
II. Thorndike Press large print romance series.
PS3619.A55S66 2005
813'.6—dc22   2005027325

Dedicated to the memory of my father
Lawrence David Dworzynski

Special thanks to
my husband, Don, my son, Anthony
my mother, Helen,
and all my brothers and sisters
for all their support;
to Dave for his *lawyer lingo;*
to my critique group,
Lynda, Maggi, Anita and Laura;
and last, but not least,
to Terry and Catherine
for supplying all the endless hours
of vacuuming that inspired this story.

As the Founder/CEO of NAVH, the only national health agency solely devoted to those who, although not totally blind, have an eye disease which could lead to serious visual impairment, I am pleased to recognize Thorndike Press★ as one of the leading publishers in the large print field.

Founded in 1954 in San Francisco to prepare large print textbooks for partially seeing children, NAVH became the pioneer and standard setting agency in the preparation of large type.

Today, those publishers who meet our standards carry the prestigious "Seal of Approval" indicating high quality large print. We are delighted that Thorndike Press is one of the publishers whose titles meet these standards. We are also pleased to recognize the significant contribution Thorndike Press is making in this important and growing field.

Lorraine H. Marchi, L.H.D.
Founder/CEO
NAVH

★ Thorndike Press encompasses the following imprints: Thorndike, Wheeler, Walker and Large Print Press.

Chapter 1

"Single?"

Come-on lines had certainly changed
since she'd been out of the dating scene,
Ginger Thompson thought. Part of her was
flattered the dark-haired, handsome man
behind her had even noticed her. The other
part of her bristled at such a forward question. "None of your business," she answered, her breath a puff of white in the
chilly morning air. She wondered if he'd ask
about her sexual preference next.

The waiting-line inched forward and she
dug her ski poles into the trampled snow-
packed ground and moved up.

The man chuckled, a deep husky sound
she immediately liked. "I wasn't asking
about your marital status, although that is a
good question." He moved right along behind her with the grace of a natural-born
skier. "I wondered if you were riding to the
top by yourself. If so, I'll share the lift with
you."

"I . . . no, I'm not going up just yet. I'm

waiting for someone." Embarrassed, Ginger sidestepped away from the single formation.

"Are you sure?"

"Very."

"Well, whoever he is, he's a lucky guy." The man winked, then moved away from her as the line surged forward.

She stood watching him. Steven was out of her life for good. She had every right to flirt with any guy she wanted to. So why couldn't she? If she didn't change her attitude toward men soon, she'd end up alone for the rest of her life. And there was no way she wanted to be like her mother. Not if she had anything to say about it.

"Lighten up, Ginger. I brought you on this ski trip for fun and excitement. You still know how to have fun, don't you?"

Ginger looked at her friend, Robyn, across the beer bottles littering the table. "Of course," she sniffed. But did she? Her reaction to the handsome man this morning had her wondering.

Robyn paused with the brown bottle halfway to her brightly painted lips. "Then prove it, woman. It's not every day I win free contest tickets, you know. We have to make the most of it. I want to see the old Ginger I used to know." She set the drink on the table and leaned forward, a lock of her dark brown hair twisting around her gold hoop earring. "We've had some great times, you and I."

The twinkle in Robyn's eyes was unmistakable and Ginger had to chuckle. "As I recall we used to get into a lot of trouble."

"Trouble . . . fun. It's all the same. We never did anything illegal. And as *I* recall, you enjoyed our little escapades as much as I did."

She remembered when she first met Robyn back in the second grade. Ginger had moved to the Denver area after the school year started. The teacher designated her as a helper and sent her back into the room to retrieve a sweater for her. As Ginger walked into the class, she spotted Robyn stuffing a frog in the lunchbox of a girl who had teased her. Robyn had convinced Ginger to pose as lookout and they had remained loyal friends ever since.

"Don't look now, but a couple of guys are checking us out."

Ginger started to turn in her chair. Not that she thought any man would be interested in a woman who didn't know how to have fun. They were probably just interested in Robyn. "Where — ?"

"Not now! We don't want them to know

we know they're looking our way. Boy, you really are rusty. Five years in a deadend relationship didn't do you any favors."

Blindly staring at the table, Ginger's heart tightened and a lump in her throat threatened to cut off her speech. "You promised you wouldn't mention Steven on this trip." It still hurt to think of him, even if she had been the one who had called it quits.

"Consider him unmentioned." Her friend reached across the table and squeezed her hand. "You're not your mother, you know."

Ginger's gaze met Robyn's. "What's that supposed to mean?"

"It's just that, well . . . I've heard your mother preach a thousand times about the evils of wicked men and how much better off we would all be without them."

"My dad did a real number on her."

"You never met him, did you?" Robyn questioned.

"No. He left before he even knew my mom was pregnant. She refused to look for him. Pride made her keep the secret to herself."

Robyn shook her head. "One bad guy shouldn't make all the rest rotten. Confess. That's why you stuck with Steven so long, isn't it? He's safe and predictable."

"Steven is a great guy," Ginger said, defensive all of a sudden.

"Yeah, yeah, yeah," Robyn agreed, waving her hands in the air. "He's great. But he's not the guy for you. You need someone more exciting, more alive. You need to get out of the boring rut you're in." She paused for a moment. "Hey, I've got a great idea."

Looking up, Ginger saw a gleam in her friend's eyes and knew it was time to panic. "Robyn Jeffries, I've seen that look before. I don't know what you're thinking, but I know I'm not going to like it."

"Dammit, Ginger. You act like your life is over when it's really just begun. You've finally rid yourself of Mr. Boring and you should have some fun."

Boring? Is that how her best friend saw Steven? Ginger thought of him more as a steadying influence. "But —"

"No buts. This weekend you are going to do everything I tell you. You are at my command. Do you understand?"

Ginger's spirits lifted a notch. Robyn was irresistible.

"Yes, master." With a smile on her face, she raised her beer bottle. "A toast . . . to fun."

They clinked their drinks together, and Robyn added, "You won't regret this, my friend. But first — the rules."

Ginger groaned. "Rules?"

"If you want to play the game you have to follow the rules."

"Rules are too complicated."

"Not these. Rule number one. You have to give your phone number to every guy who asks for it."

Panic flooded Ginger. "You've got to be crazy. Don't you read the papers?"

"Of course I do. Calm yourself. I have the perfect solution." Reaching into her purse, Robyn fished around for a moment and pulled out a pen.

Robyn toyed with it. "This is filled with disappearing ink. I took it from my kid brother. You just have to *give* every guy your phone number. I didn't say they would go home with it."

Ginger shook her head. "You never cease to amaze me. All right. What's rule number two?"

"Eager now, are we?" Robyn dropped the pen back into her purse and settled into her chair. "Okay. Rule number two . . . we have to have great careers."

"We do have great careers. You own your own company and I —"

"I own a janitorial service. I clean high-rise office buildings. While I've worked hard for my business and I'm proud of how far I've gotten, cleaning up after other people's

12

messes isn't exactly glamorous. I've always wanted to be . . . a flight attendant."

"All five-foot-one-and-a-half inches of you?"

"So I'm a little short. Most of these guys are half crocked anyway. They'll never notice a little technicality like height. Now for you." Robyn cocked her head sideways and studied her best friend through squinted eyes.

Fidgeting in her seat, Ginger felt like a bug on the end of a pin. "Knock it off, you're making me nervous."

"We don't have to change your career too much, since you're a secretary at a modeling agency. We'll just make you a model."

Ginger slammed her bottle on the table top. Beer splashed onto the Formica surface. "No way. I will not pretend I'm a model."

"Why not? I've always thought you were prettier than most of them. With your perfect blond hair and take-me-to-bed blue eyes, you're a knockout."

Ginger knew she couldn't do it. And it had nothing to do with her looks. "I could never pull it off. I don't have a model's . . . er . . . temperament."

Robyn started to laugh. "Temperament?" she managed to get out.

"Fine." It wasn't like it was a well-kept secret. "You remember my senior class nickname. 'Class Klutz — Most likely to collide' will follow me to the day I die." The title still stung.

"We're just pretending here, Gin."

"Do I need to remind you what happened the last time I *pretended* to be a model?" The memory still embarrassed her.

"It's not your fault you almost broke that photographer's camera. He's the one who told you to spin."

Ginger grimaced. "My ears still burn from his French oaths."

"God, I wish I could have been there." Robyn's sigh filled the space between them. "Well, I promise, you're not going to have to pose in front of a camera or walk down a runway."

"Doesn't matter. This isn't going to work."

"Sure it is. All five-feet-eight, 36–24–36 of you is going to be a model for the weekend. Do you hear and obey?"

Oh, brother. Robyn would wear her down eventually. She might as well give in now. Ginger agreed though she wasn't quite sure her heart was in it. "All right, all right," she swung her hands in the air. Her wrist made contact with a beer bottle and to her mortification, sent it flying off the table. It was an omen, she thought as Robyn burst into more peals of laughter. "I'm going to live to regret this. My mother always said liars never prosper."

"Your mother says a lot of things. And we're not lying, we're just . . . embellishing. Speaking of *embellishing*, we need to change our last names . . . to protect the innocent, of course."

"Of course. What do you have in mind for me?"

"You can use my mother's maiden name. Cooper."

"Ginger Cooper it is. And you can be . . . Robyn Banks." If she had to sound refined, her friend should sound like a criminal.

Robyn held her head sideways. "That is so cute. I love it. You're starting to get the hang of this embellishing stuff."

"Great. I'll put it on my resumé next time I'm in the market for a new job. Dare I ask for rule number three?"

"Sorry, woman. You don't get rule number three until tomorrow. I don't want to shock your system beyond repair."

Ginger felt a sudden sense of longing for the comfortable relationship she had shared with Steven before she told him she wanted out. Meeting new men was unfamiliar and a little scary. "I'm too old for this, Robyn."

"Twenty-nine is not too old. Relax. Look at all these men. You should be having as much fun as a puppy in a hydrant factory."

Leave it to Robyn to sum everything up so eloquently.

"Wow. Challenge number one just walked into the room. I was standing at the front desk when he checked in. Definitely your type. You liked dark-haired guys in high school and college. Now what did he say his name was?" She clicked her fingers. "Vince something or other. It was an Italian name. He's in the penthouse suite, so he must be rich."

Turning in her seat, Ginger surveyed the crowd nonchalantly. Then she saw him leaning against the end of the bar.

She gasped, her heart beating rapidly inside her chest like the wings of a humming-bird. It was the man who'd spoken to her at the ski lift, looking drop-dead gorgeous in blue jeans and a black sweater. He seemed utterly sure of himself, powerfully sensual, and very out of her league.

Spinning back in her seat, she took a quick swallow of her beer. Robyn grinned wickedly.

"Sexy, ain't he?"

"Yes. And we both know what my mother says about sexy men."

"A sexy man is a dangerous man," they both piped in unison.

For once she knew what her mother meant. He reminded her of a panther seeking prey. She'd felt it this morning. She could feel it now from across the room. He had already taken her breath away and she had only *looked* at him.

Trying to appear casual, she turned, pretending to watch couples two-stepping on the dance floor to a country tune. Helpless to stop it, her gaze shifted back to the man at the end of the bar.

He was temptation personified. And as if Ginger's mom sat next to her whispering in her ear, she could hear her words. *Oh, no, Ginger. He's too much of a man. Stay away from him. He'll only end up hurting you. All men end up hurting women. Mark my words. It's inevitable.*

But, like a woman ravenous after following a diet for too long, Ginger devoured his body with her eyes. Her stare traced the incredible length of his well-defined, muscular legs to the tips of his cowboy boots.

Traveling back up she assessed the wide expanse of his chest hidden beneath that black sweater.

Her gaze traveled higher. She studied a sensuous set of lips, which curved into a slow grin revealing a dimple in one cheek. Her look shot up higher and she stared straight into eyes that she remembered were green. The man tipped his drink to her in a mock salute.

Embarrassed to have been caught studying him so openly, she spun around in her chair, her heart somersaulting in her chest, her cheeks burning. "Oh, my God. He caught me looking at him." Was this the part where she was supposed to be having fun?

"I'm sure you're not the first woman to ever look at him," Robyn drawled.

"No. You don't understand. I mean he caught me *really* looking a him. Every part of him."

"Oh, you mean you were staring at his —"

Ginger didn't like the grin on her friend's face. Irritation triggered sarcasm. "You read too many romances."

"You don't read enough." Robyn's laughter echoed around her. "Rule number one just changed. Instead of giving every guy your phone number, you have to get him to ask you out on the slopes tomorrow."

Ginger rubbed her temples. "I have a headache."

Robyn fished in her purse again and set a bottle of tablets on the table. "Then take some aspirin. You've got work to do."

The chair next to Ginger was pulled away from the table as a brown-haired, attractive man sat down. "Hello, little lady," he said to Robyn. "I noticed you from across the room and couldn't stop myself from coming over." He jabbed a thumb toward the dance floor. "Wanna dance?"

He held out his hand and Robyn took it. "I'd love to." Rising from her chair she leaned toward Ginger. "Get ready," she whispered in her ear. "He's coming this way."

Ginger felt the blood drain from her face. She closed her eyes and swallowed her fear. When she opened them again, she could feel him standing there. His presence was almost tangible, and overpowering. It made the hairs on her neck tingle. Slowly she turned her head and looked into his laughing green eyes.

"Dance with me."

It wasn't a question, she noticed. It was a challenge — one she felt absolutely powerless to refuse.

Without a word, Ginger rose from her chair and followed his lead to the middle of the dance floor. A slow song crooned from the speakers placed about the room. Ginger inwardly groaned. Slow songs meant one thing.

Close contact.

He drew her toward him with his eyes as well as his hands. A muscular arm wrapped about her waist. Embarrassment washed over her. Ginger stared at his chin instead. He guided her about the room, her body pressed close to his.

Too damned close.

Ginger laughed to herself. She was taking this too seriously. Wasn't she? This was just a dance. When the weekend was over, this man would be out of her life forever, and forgotten.

Ginger caught Robyn's eye. Her friend winked at her and a smile tugged at Ginger's lips.

"You should do that more often."

Startled, Ginger looked up at him. "Do what?"

"Smile."

Heat rushed to her cheeks and she turned her gaze away from the bold, appraising look in his eyes. Even his voice gave her the shivers. What was happening to her?

"What's your name?"

"Ginger. Um . . ." What was her new last

20

name again? "Ginger Cooper. Don't tell me yours," she said, suddenly remembering Robyn had overheard his name earlier. "Let me guess."

"Guess away."

She leaned her head to one side as if studying the handsome lines of his face would give her a clue. "You definitely can't be a Bill or a George."

"Right on both counts."

"How about Larry or Frank?"

"Nope."

"Sam, then. Or maybe . . . Vince."

A startled look flashed in his eyes. "How did you know?"

"A woman has her ways."

He laughed throatily and drew her even closer; then rested his chin on top of her head.

For a few moments, they danced in silence while Ginger relished the warmth of Vince's embrace. She felt as if she had been in his arms before and belonged there now. She closed her eyes and rested her cheek on his chest, comforted by the rhythmic beating of his heart.

"Do you believe in fate, Ginger?"

The abrupt question caused her to pull away. She took the chance of staring into his eyes. Fate? As if she *had* known this man before? As if destiny had brought them together again? It simply wasn't possible. "No, I don't."

"You will."

He sounded so sure of himself that Ginger knew he actually believed what he'd said. She swallowed hard.

She knew he was going to kiss her before he even made a move. She wanted him to — wanted to feel his lips against hers. She had to know if his kiss felt as familiar as his arms about her waist. With the music still playing, they stopped. Together they stood motionless amongst all the other dancers.

His head dipped lower and lower until his lips found hers. Gently at first, his tongue edged her mouth open and demanded entrance.

Ginger closed her eyes, as helpless as an animal caught in the coils of a snake. Her knees grew weak. If he hadn't been holding her so tight, she probably would have collapsed on the floor.

Vince broke the kiss and pulled away.

Ginger longed to run her fingers through his thick black hair and pull his warm mouth back to hers. She looked into his eyes, an unmistakable passion burning in their depths. Why had he stopped kissing her? She sensed he had enjoyed it as much as she had, and wondered what style of lover he would be.

Embarrassed at the path of her imagination, she looked away. The shock of what she'd done slammed into her. Was she about to become another notch on his bedpost because she couldn't say no to Robyn? She wasn't sure she could say no to him.

He came.

He saw.

He conquered.

Not if she had anything to say about it!

They resumed dancing. Stumbling, Ginger trod heavily on the toe of his boot. "Sorry," she apologized, shooting a look at his face. It didn't seem to bother him in the least.

"Would you like to sit down?" he asked.

Ginger nodded, not trusting her voice.

Vince held out her chair and then took the one next to it. To her relief, he didn't pull his seat too close. He seemed to realize she needed space and decided to give it to her.

With her usual tact, Robyn chose that moment to return to the table. She held out her hand across the Formica to Vince. "Hi. I'm Robyn."

Vince grabbed her hand and shook it. "I'm Vince. Would you two ladies like a drink?"

"A couple of beers would be great," Robyn said.

"Don't go away." He winked at Ginger. "I'll be right back."

She watched him disappear into the crowd surrounding the bar.

Robyn watched him, too. "Yum. He is a sight to behold." She turned toward Ginger. "Hey, you two looked as hot as a fireman's helmet out there. I thought the floor was going to melt out from under you."

Heat rushed into Ginger's cheeks. Had everyone been watching? "I . . . I don't know what came over me," she stammered, embarrassed at her passionate public display.

"Lust came over you. Bet you never felt that way with good old what's-his-name."

No, Steven had never made her feel that way. She had never felt that way with anyone. She had known this man all of five minutes and she couldn't contain herself. She felt hot all over and flustered. This foolishness had to stop here and now.

"Did he ask you to go skiing tomorrow?"

Ginger shrugged her shoulders. "We didn't do much talking."

Before Robyn could make any caustic remarks, Vince came back to the table and set down three beers.

"So what brings you ladies to Steamboat?"

"A little skiing and —"

"A little skiing is all," Ginger interrupted, sending Robyn a dirty look. No telling what she was about to say.

"Do you live in Colorado, Vince?" Robyn asked.

Ginger didn't mind her friend doing most of the talking. With Vince's leg brushing against hers, thinking coherently — let alone speaking — seemed an unrealistic goal.

"I'm moving to Denver from Washington, D.C. in a couple of weeks."

"Wow. What are you, a senator or something?"

He laughed. "No. Just a business executive. What about you?"

Ginger looked up to find his green eyes trained on her. She felt glad now that she and Robyn had readymade lies. It saved her from having to come up with one. "I'm a model." She didn't even trip over the fib though it tasted nasty in her mouth.

Robyn gave her a thumbs-up sign on their side of the table, hidden from Vince's eyes, which Ginger chose to ignore.

"With a face and figure like yours, I should have guessed. Will I see you on any magazine covers?" His eyes appraised her body boldly, sending shivers to parts of her she didn't even know existed.

"No. I only just started . . . not too long ago." Ginger averted her gaze. *Ten minutes to be exact.*

"My goodness, look at the time," Robyn said. "I need my beauty sleep." Scraping back her chair, she got up from the table. "Nice meeting you, Vince. I'll see you later, Gin."

Before Ginger could sputter an objection, her friend was gone. Panic roared inside her. She took a swift gulp of beer to hide her nervousness. Robyn didn't even have the decency to stick around and help her out of this mess. She wanted to yell at her that paybacks were hell, but Robyn was already gone.

How could she say anything intelligent when her tongue was tied in knots? Good Lord, Ginger chided herself. He's human. I can make conversation. She peeked at him through her lashes. No doubt about it. She was a mere human. And he was a god.

"I won't bite."

A cocky, self-assured god.

"Promise?"

He laughed huskily, the sound sending delicious shivers throughout her body. "Maybe a nibble here and there."

His muscular thigh brushed against hers. Even as she fought it, a little thrill of excitement traveled through her system. He was everything her mother had warned her about and then some. Reaching for her purse, ready to flee, Ginger glanced in his direction one last time. Those damned devil-may-care eyes drew her in against her will.

A nibble or two couldn't hurt.

He turned sideways to watch the dancers and Ginger took the opportunity to study his face. Bold, angular lines defined a strong jaw. His full lips opened in a sudden smile and those dangerous eyes looked toward her again. Vince flashed her a smile so devastatingly sexy it almost knocked her off her chair. If she didn't know better, she would think her mother had sent him.

He was a test.

Of the emergency heartbreak system.

One batting of the eyelashes, one innocent flutter of her heart indicated failure. She had to get away from his provocative smile, kissable dimple, and mesmerizing eyes before it was too late. She placed her hands on the edge of the table to push her chair away. "It's been nice meeting you, Vince, but I need to get to bed."

"Is that an invitation?"

Was it too late already? She dredged up the courage that had sunk to somewhere between her toes. "Look, you're a nice guy." *A very handsome, sexy, desirable, nice guy and I'll kick myself later for turning you down.* "But I'm just not that kind of girl."

His eyes narrowed. He took a sip of his beer as if prolonging his answer.

"Fine. We'll play the game your way."

Ginger stopped. Game? She hated games. She had a hard time winning. "My way?"

"I'll court you."

He sure had a high opinion of himself. Suppose she didn't want to court him? "Look, Mr. — ?"

"Danelli. But call me Vince."

"Look, Mr. Danelli, I don't play games. I don't wish to be seen with, courted by or . . . or seduced by the likes of you." *Liar.*

His gaze branded her from across the table. "Sometimes you don't get what you want. You get what you need." His words came out lazily, as if he enjoyed every minute of his verbal foreplay.

Indignation flared. "Of all the —"

"Face it, Ginger Cooper." He grabbed her hand and rubbed his thumb seductively across her palm. "There are some things in life you just can't fight. What's happening between us — what could happen between us — is one of those things."

She wanted to deny his words. But with the electricity flowing from his fingers into her hand, down her arm, and from there, flooding her entire nervous system, it was pointless. She stood rooted to the spot, staring into his eyes. The man was right. She couldn't fight him. Not even the cavalry could save her now.

"I'll see you at 9:00 a.m. tomorrow. Consider it our first date." His warm lips seared a kiss on the top of her hand, then he left.

He hadn't asked, Ginger noticed, if she even *wanted* to go on a date with him. For the second time that night she felt as if he had issued a challenge. Well, she'd meet his damn challenge, she vowed. And win.

The man watched the woman from his corner across the room. So far, so good. But he knew better than to get his hopes up. Vince Danelli was almost as cunning as he was. Almost. But no one outsmarted Renard Duchaine twice.

No one.

"Hey, boss, this is going better than we expected."

"Keep your voice down," he said, turning an angry look on the fair-haired man sliding his small frame onto the seat across from him. "Do you want the whole world to know what we're up to, Johnson?"

"No one will know," the man whispered.

He was right. The plan was progressing better than he had expected or hoped. He'd wanted the Jeffries woman to be seen by Danelli. Never in his wildest dreams had he imagined her friend would attract him. The women were setting themselves up and they didn't even know it.

He looked in the mirror above the bar and stretched his lips into a thin smile. He wanted to laugh. The payback for Vince stealing his family and his woman was starting to fall into place. Hell, he was so happy at this point he could have cried.

"She's leaving, boss."

"Follow her. And Johnson . . ."

"Yeah?"

"Don't let her see you."

Chapter 2

"Am I paranoid? Or is that guy following me?" Ginger looked over her shoulder at a shadowy corner of the lobby, apprehension gnawing at her.

"Where? Who?" Robyn asked.

"There." She pointed. "Now he's gone." Ginger frowned. Was her mind playing tricks on her?

"What does he look like?"

"I don't know. Pretty average, I guess. I haven't been able to get that close a look. Every time I turn around, I see the back of him turning a corner or something. I think he was following me last night, too." A tingle of anxiety quivered down Ginger's spine.

Robin shrugged. "Well, you know it isn't Vince. He's anything but average-looking. When are you meeting him?"

Ginger's stomach did a double reverse belly flop. "I'm not," she insisted. "I'm going skiing. If he happens to be there, fine. If not, I'm spending the day on the bunny slope anyway. I'm such a klutzy skier, I'll probably knock him down. Where are you meeting what's-his-name again?"

"Rick? By the ski rental place." Robyn glanced at her watch. "Do you want to meet for lunch?"

"Sure. How about noon in the hotel restaurant?"

"Fine."

The crisp early December air greeted them as they walked out of the hotel. A fresh layer of snow glittered on the ground under the bright morning sun. Ginger reached for her tinted goggles to cut the harsh glare.

After renting skis, she waved goodbye to her friend and merged into the lift line.

Behind her, a skier came to a sudden stop sending a crystalline spray of snow all over her red parka.

"Hey!" she yelled with a glance over her shoulder.

Vince Danelli stood within touching distance. He wore a black parka and jeans that hugged every well-defined muscle. His smile chiseled away at her cool resolve to remain detached from his obvious charms.

The way Ginger's heart raced in her chest at the mere sight of the man irritated her. She scowled at him. She wasn't ready to admit to herself she was glad he was there.

"Didn't we have a date?" he asked.

"The only date I have, Danelli, is with this bunny hill." She refused to turn around. He was too handsome for his own good, and too handsome for her own peace of mind.

"The bunny hill it is then." He filed in behind her.

Ginger gritted her teeth. The man really couldn't take a hint. Finally at the top, she congratulated herself on not tripping over her own skis getting off the lift. A blast of frigid air whipped around her, scented with pine trees. Ginger shivered. She had never been much of a skier. Robyn had talked her into this vacation, even though she hated cold weather and she hated speed. What the hell was she doing on top of a mountain anyway?

Vince stopped next to her and adjusted the goggles over his eyes. "Wanna race?"

Tearing her gaze from the dimple in his cheek, she glanced down the hill. What had looked like an innocent bunny slope from the bottom now looked like Mount Everest. And she was supposed to descend it? Without falling? "Sure. I'll give you a headstart."

"Ladies first," he said.

"No. I insist." *Please, nobody, and I do mean nobody, in the world needs to witness my wonderful skiing ability.*

"*That* good, are you?"

"You've never seen anything like it."
Ginger watched him swish down the hill
with the skill of an expert. "Figures," she
muttered. With her poles digging into the
white powder, she pushed off the hill and
started her downward descent. Her speed
started off slow. *This isn't so bad,* she
thought, elated at her skill so far. *I could
easily get the hang of this.* Then the trees
on either side began to rush by in a green
blur. Fear raced in her chest as fast as she
raced down the hill.

Vince stopped halfway down and looked
up. "Snowplow!" he yelled.

Snowplow? What the hell did that mean?
Oh, my God! Was there one following her?
She couldn't get out of the way if she tried.
With her heart beating wildly and the tips of
her skis aimed right at him, she had no
choice but to follow their lead. In mere seconds she would mow him down in cold
blood.

Get out of the way, she wanted to scream,
but the words froze on her lips. Ginger saw
surprise and realization leap into his eyes
the instant before she hit him. The impact
sent them tumbling to the ground, twisting
together in a jumble of arms, legs, and skis,
like a human snowball.

When they finally stopped, Ginger lay

prone, her chest heaving. Her goggles slanted across her nose and one eye. Vince lay on top of her, gasping for breath.

"Are you hurt?" he asked.

"Just my pride."

"I keep trying to tell you you've swept me off my feet, Cooper. Do you believe me now?"

She looked into the handsome face mere inches from hers. Ginger bit her lip. She refused to succumb to his charms.

"No. I *don't* believe you. Now get off me, you big lug." She pushed at his massive shoulders.

Never taking his gaze off Ginger, he untangled his limbs from hers and clambered to his feet. Green eyes glinted colder than the chunk of snow sneaking its way up the back of her sweater.

"I'm sorry," he said. "I mistook you for a woman who responded to me last night. I don't know what I've done to offend you, but I know when I'm not wanted."

With a decisive click, he snapped his boots back onto his skis. "You need skiing lessons. You're dangerous." Without looking back, he continued on down the mountain.

"I'm dangerous?" she yelled, grabbing a fistful of snow and whipping it in his general direction. "You're the one threatening my sanity!" With a groan she fell back on the snow and laid her forearm over her eyes. *What have I done? What harm could possibly come from spending the day with a man I'm wildly attracted to?*

"Ma'am, are you okay?"

Ginger peeked from behind her arm to see a middle-aged man dressed in a red and white ski patrol jacket staring at her with concern in his eyes.

"No. I'm not okay." She sat up. "I'm a stupid, stupid idiot." The man stared at her. "I let him ski away from me. Why did I let him get away?"

"I don't know."

"Tell me I should go after him."

"You should go after him."

She could see the skepticism in the man's eyes. He thought she was a nut, but she was beyond caring what anyone thought. She wanted him to respond, even though she already knew what the answer would be. "Why should I go after him?"

"Because you like him?"

"You're right. I do. And I will. Right after you help me off this blasted mountain."

Damn woman! Vince thought. One minute she's staring at me with deep-blue come-and-get-me bedroom eyes and the next she's giving me the cold shoulder. They should all come with a warning label.

After the number his lying, cheating ex-wife had done on him, it was a wonder he wanted anything to do with women at all.

Taking off his skis, he jabbed the tips into the snow and smiled to himself. He learned something from his sham of a marriage. He'd learned how to use women and toss them aside before he got hurt. Taking off his glove, he bent over to adjust the clasp on his boot.

"Woaaaahhhh. Look out!"

Two hands planted on his rear and knocked him to the ground. With a thud, a body fell on top of him. A soft body. A woman's body. Vince glared over his shoulder at his assailant.

Ginger, wearing a sheepish grin, stared back. "Imagine running into you like this."

He smelled her perfume, envisioned he could feel her breasts pressing against his back even through all their thick clothes. With a growl, Vince stood and sent her soft feminine form rolling off him. Her skis had popped off in the fall and she landed on top of them. "You're bound and determined to break some part of me, aren't you?"

"It was an accident. Honest." She held up

her fingers in the Girl Scout salute. "These skis have a mind of their own."

She looked so innocent sitting on the frigid ground in her red parka, her shoulder-length hair a wild halo about her face. Innocent and irresistible. He reached out a hand to help her up. After a slight hesitation, Ginger placed thick gloved fingers in his. With one tug, Vince drew her into his embrace, and a delicate flush danced on her cheeks.

She doesn't want you, bud. Does she have to reject you twice in one day before it sinks into your thick skull?

She fit perfectly within the circle of his arms, and against every emotion stirring inside him, he released her. Scooping up her poles, Vince placed them in her gloved hand. "If you hurry, there's still time for you to sign up for a morning lesson."

"I'm ready when you are."

Vince tensed. A muscle ticked in his jaw. The truth hit him like the proverbial ton of bricks. He wanted her more than he'd ever wanted any woman. "I'm not interested." Yeah, right.

"I'm not . . . look, we got off on the wrong foot. I'm sorry. It's all my fault, I admit it. Can we start over?" Without waiting for his answer, she stuck out her hand. "Hi. My name's Ginger."

He stood with his hands on his hips and ignored her outstretched arm. If he touched her, it would be his undoing. Running a hand through his hair in agitation, he conceded. "All right, I'll give you a lesson. But only because it's safer to have you in front of me than behind."

Her answering smile illuminated her face and Vince's breath caught in his throat. This woman could tempt the devil. And he was no saint. He grabbed his skis and put them back on. "Do you think you could make it to the top without harming anyone in your path?" he asked, sarcasm dripping from his voice. Maybe if he was rude to her, she'd go away.

She raised one perfectly arched eyebrow. "Of course. Going up is a piece of cake. Getting down is where I have the problem."

"So I've noticed."

Putting her skis back on, Ginger executed an awkward turn, and Vince had to bite the inside of his cheek to keep from laughing. How had a woman as uncoordinated as this ever become a model? He answered his own question as he followed her to the lift. Her body. Even through her padded outfit, her hour-glass figure taunted him. His mouth watered to taste her lips again. His loins tightened with the need to possess her. With the woman's *look, but don't touch* attitude, giving a lesson would be a definite trip to the gates of hell.

Too busy watching her hips sway from side to side, Vince didn't notice his skis cross at the tips until it was too late. The movement caught him off guard and he pitched forward, planting his face in a cold drift.

He heard Ginger laughing above him. Vince tried glaring at her, but even he could see the humor in the situation. He chuckled grudgingly. "Cooper, you'll be the death of me yet."

"I didn't touch you, Danelli. And please don't call me Cooper."

Honey, you don't need to touch me to distract me beyond all reason.

"I am rethinking this lesson thing, though. Maybe I do need the assistance of a professional."

He growled deep in his throat. *Maybe that's a good idea. Out of sight, out of mind.* Vince sent her one of his best dimpled grins, the kind that, in the past, had always won the hearts of unsuspecting women. "Don't even think it, Cooper. No professional alive can teach you what I know." *And I'm not talking about skiing.*

Pushing himself up from the ground, he stood. "The first skill you need to learn is how to stop. For my safety and for anyone foolish enough to ski anywhere near you."

She frowned. "I'm not that bad."

He shot her a scathing look, but didn't comment. Her actions spoke louder than words. "The easiest way for a beginner to stop is to snowplow."

"Snowplow refers to stopping?"

"Of course. What did you think it meant?"

A bright red flush stained her cheeks that had nothing to do with the cold weather.

"It's not important," she muttered.

He moved to her side. "All you have to do is point the tips of your skis together like this." He demonstrated.

Her gloved hand reached out and brushed snow off his cheek with a lingering, delicate touch. His gaze shot to hers, searching for an answer, a clue to her real feelings. He felt himself start to harden just from that simple caress. God, she was desirable.

"Thanks, Vince."

He wanted to kiss her. No, not just kiss her, devour her. She made him feel awkward and out of control, like a sixteen-year-old schoolboy. Blood pulsed in his veins. He ignored it. "Are you paying attention?"

Ginger flashed him a smile. "I heard every word. All I have to do is point the tips together, like this." With a swish, she landed on her butt. "Maybe you'd better show me that move again."

An hour and many attempts later, they finally reached the bottom of the hill. "I did it, Vince. I did it!"

He smiled.

She smiled back.

He had to give her credit. Anyone else would have given up long ago. The woman didn't complain. She had to be frozen from landing in the snow so many times, but she never uttered a negative word. "I think you deserve a reward." He grabbed the end of her scarf and with his own skis spread wide, pulled her toward him, one slow, tantalizing inch at a time.

Her blue eyes grew wide, and her lips parted.

She wanted him, he realized with a start. As much as he wanted her.

And he would make her admit it before the day ended. With Ginger so close, he could swear he heard her heart beating. Vince held out his hand and grabbing hers, he shook it. "Good job," he said. "Now let's get back up on top and begin lesson number two."

"You have to bend into the turns," Vince told her for the hundredth time.

The man, Ginger decided, had the patience of a saint. "I'm trying."

"Move your hips. Pretend you're walking down the runway at a fashion show. Like this." He swished his hips in an exaggerated manner.

Ginger laughed. "My, you have real potential. Maybe *you* ought to become a model."

"Very funny. Try it again. Move your hips."

Wiggling in a manner she knew in no way resembled what she was supposed to do, she sighed in exasperation. "I can't get this." Should she tell him now that it was hopeless — that she was about as coordinated as a fish on rollerskates? That she wore the crown of "Class Klutz?"

Vince came up behind her, his skis on the outside of hers. Large, masculine hands grabbed her hips. She thought she would melt at the touch.

"Move this way," he whispered, his breath warm against her neck, his hard chest pressing against her back.

He shifted her about in a seductive way that had nothing to do with skiing. Ginger licked her lips anxiously and looked at the gorgeous hunk of man behind her. "Are you sure that's how it's done?" she murmured.

"Trust me."

She saw a glint in his eyes, and an irresistibly boyish grin. He meant, trust me as a man. Should she? Did she have the guts? Ginger swallowed down her nervousness. "My goodness, look at the time." No sense telling him she wasn't wearing a watch. "I promised I'd meet Robyn for lunch. Care to join us?"

"Chicken."

"What?"

"I hope they have chicken." His dimple appeared when he smiled at her. "I'm hungry."

Ginger snowplowed at a snail's pace down the length of the hill with Vince trailing a safe distance behind. He still refused to get in front of her. After resting their skis against a rack, the touch of Vince's hand at the small of her back propelled her toward the lodge.

Grabbing a spot next to the roaring fireplace, they shed their coats. His long legs caged hers under the table, and the chill lingering in her bones evaporated. Warmth, more from his nearness than the flames in the hearth, enveloped her.

"Should we get an appetizer while we wait for Robyn?"

"I'm not an appetizer kind of guy."

Her eyes shot to his. Why did his words always seem to hold a hidden meaning?

"I much prefer the main course."

Oh, God. Ginger felt like a sacrificial lamb. And Vince looked hungry. Real hungry.

A movement by the entrance tore her gaze from his. Robyn waved to her from across the room. The man named Rick stood by her side. When Robyn pointed out Ginger and Vince, an agitated look flashed across Rick's face. From where Ginger sat, it looked like they were arguing. It was over in a second and with an airy wave from Robyn, the two left.

"That's strange," Ginger whispered half to herself before turning back to Vince.

"What?"

Rick's attitude left Ginger with an uneasy feeling in the pit of her stomach. She tried to shrug it off. "Robyn and her friend . . ."

"Yeah?"

"I thought they were going to join us, but then they left."

"Good." His wolfish smile revealed his true intentions. "That means I get you all to myself."

After lunch they returned to the top of the slope for more of lesson number two. By the time the winter sun started to fade into the mountains, Ginger longed to call it quits.

She couldn't feel her fingers or her toes and as tired as she felt, she didn't care.

Crawling to her room would have been easier than walking. Vince must have sensed her exhaustion. He slipped a strong arm about her waist and all but carried her toward the hotel. His nearness, more than the exercise, left her breathless.

"Just send me in the direction of my room. I'm going to fall on my bed and stay there for a week."

"Oh, no, you're not."

"Please," she begged, too numb and exhausted to say more.

"If you lie down now your muscles will tighten up and you'll feel like hell tomorrow."

"I feel like hell right now."

His lips twitched. "It'll get worse." The elevator whisked them to her floor and Vince stopped at the door to her room. "Get your swimsuit and meet me at the hot tub in ten minutes."

"But —"

"No buts." He tucked a loose strand of hair behind her ear. "You did great today. I'm proud of you." Bending, his lips touched hers in a gentle kiss.

A tremble shook Ginger's body. Her heart thundered in her chest. She wanted more.

"Ten minutes," he whispered. Running a feather-light touch down her cheek, he turned and strode to the elevator.

His musky scent lingering in the hallway with her, Ginger pressed trembling fingers to her lips as she leaned back against the doorway. Lost in her thoughts, she had no warning when the door burst open behind her and she spilled into the room.

"I thought I heard someone out there," Robyn said, looking down at her roommate.

From her location on the floor, Ginger shot her friend a weary glance. Landing on her butt for the two hundredth time didn't sooth her sore, tired muscles. "Help me up," she muttered.

Robyn took her hand. "What's the matter with you?"

"This skiing stuff is hard work. I ache everywhere," she moaned.

"You ought to go soak in the hot tub," Robyn pulled her up from the plush, beige colored carpet.

"I'm meeting Vince down there in ten minutes." Her brows met. "Hey, what happened at lunch? Why did you and your friend leave?"

"Rick's so romantic," Robyn stated with a dreamy look in her brown eyes. "He said he didn't want to share me with anyone. What a guy. I think I'll keep this one for a little while."

"That's great," Ginger groaned. She made her way over to her suitcase and pulled out a one-piece bathing suit.

Robyn followed on her heels. "You're not going to wear *that,* are you?"

The blue and white nautical suit was modestly cut. "What's the matter with it?" she asked. The indignation in her voice sent a smirk to Robyn's lips.

"My grandmother has antiques younger than that."

"Other than going naked," Ginger asked dryly, "what do you suggest?"

A sparkle gleamed in Robyn's eyes. "Why, I'm glad you asked. I believe we'll make this rule number three."

Ginger sank onto the edge of the bed, too weary to take the news standing up. "What?"

"You're going to wear my suit." With a flourish, Robyn pulled the garment out of her bag.

"That," Ginger sputtered, fear trampling her modest sense of decency, "is not a suit. It's string . . . held together by more string."

"Hey, I'm not asking you to wear a thong suit or anything. Humor me. Try it on." She whipped the wisp of nothing onto Ginger's lap.

"White? Why in the world did you get this color? Everything, and I do mean everything, shows through when white gets wet."

Robyn smiled with the innocence of a nun. "Of course it does. Why do you think I bought it?"

"Oh, God. Why do I let you talk me into these things?" This would be the last time she ever listened to Robyn.

"Because that's what friends are for."

Ginger stripped out of her ski clothes and put on the offending two-piece in the bathroom. As she looked in the mirror, heat flooded her cheeks. Her breasts all but overflowed out of the top. In her estimation, it was at least ten sizes too small. "I can't do this," she yelled through the closed door.

"You have no choice," came the answer.

With a sigh, Ginger walked out of the bathroom.

"Wow! Va-va-va-voom. God, I wish I had big boobs like yours," Robyn said, glancing down at her own shirt front with a sigh.

"No, you don't."

"Yes, I do." Robyn pulled her blouse tight over her own breasts and frowned. "Trust me, I do."

Grabbing a T-shirt, Ginger ignored her friend and pulled it over her head. "I'll wear your stupid, indecent excuse for a suit, but no one says I have to take this cover-up off."

An appalled look flashed over Robyn's face as she stared at the 'Skier's do it on the slopes' T-shirt. "Yes, you do."

"No, I don't." Ginger stood resolute in the middle of the floor.

"Oh, yes, you do."

"No, I don't."

"Ginger."

"Robyn."

"You better or I'll never forgive you." A childish pout formed on her friend's lips.

"See ya later." With an airy wave and a "you'll never know" smile on her face, Ginger snatched a towel off the rack and left the room. On the way down, her stomach plummeted with the elevator. The closer she got to the hot tub, the slower, more measured her steps became. Her nerves took over and she wiped sweaty palms on the white T-shirt she wore.

A door with a gold-embossed "Hot Tub" sign beckoned Ginger to enter. Taking a deep breath, she pushed it open. The sound of churning bubbles, the smell of chlorine and the steam rising off the water assailed her senses. The room stood empty.

Relief, overpowering and very welcome, rippled over her. If she took her cover-up off now and got into the tub, Vince wouldn't see her pathetic excuse for a suit. Grabbing the bottom of the shirt, she pulled it over her head and tossed it on a wooden bench lining one wall.

She stood for a second testing the hot water with her toe when she felt an electrical awareness that someone was watching her. She turned slowly to face the door.

Vince leaned against the jamb wearing nothing but a pair of navy blue trunks. His arms crossed a set of pecs that could only be described as spectacular. Even in the middle of winter, he sported a slight tan. Muscles rippled across a chest sprinkled with dark hair. Appreciation flickered in his fixed stare.

Ginger swallowed.

Like a predator, he advanced, his gaze never leaving hers.

He crossed behind her, so close she could feel the heat from his body, rounded the pool and stood on the other side. Mist swirled between them.

As much as Ginger had protested to Robyn about wearing the white scrap of material, no one could make her do something against her will. She wanted Vince to look at her; wanted to see the hunger expressed in his eyes; wanted him to want her. A thrill of

51

excitement tore through her scantily clad body.

But a man as self-assured as this one was dangerous. Ginger couldn't let him know she desired him, yearned for him, longed with every fiber in her being for Vince to wrap his devastatingly sexy body around hers and never let go. No, it was his job to figure that part out for himself.

"Let's get one thing straight, Danelli," she raised her voice over the pulsing jets of the hot tub.

His eyebrows arched over green eyes that gleamed with more than a passing interest.

"I am not," she stated, "the main course."

"You're right, Cooper. You're not."

Chapter 3

Vince's deep voice rumbled across the steam escaping from the swirling, therapeutic waters. "You're the appetizer, the main course and dessert all rolled into one delicious dish."

Vince's eyes took in all of Ginger from across the tub. If he stood any closer to her, he'd come unglued. He'd guessed the layers of her clothes hid a beautiful body. Never in his wildest dreams had he foreseen the image of perfection standing in front of him now. His fingers ached to touch her and he tightened them into fists. Firm, lush, well-rounded breasts topped a slim waist curving down to long, long legs.

The white bikini, clinging like a second layer, only emphasized the creaminess of her skin. The mere sight of the woman could drive a man insane with longing. And he felt good and ready to be committed.

He watched her gaze down into the frothing depths of the water. Her natural, unaffected modesty only intensified his craving. Knowing he had better get certain parts of himself underneath the water before she discovered just how much he wanted her, Vince entered the tub.

"Come on in," he invited. They were alone. Which was exactly how he wanted it, and exactly how he'd planned it.

"Where is everybody?" she hedged. "I thought this place would be packed."

"I paid them to stay away." He couldn't take his eyes off her. Damned beautiful was the only way to describe her. Damned lucky was the only way to describe him.

"Yeah, right. Am I supposed to believe that?" Ginger chuckled.

"Honey, I've never been more serious in my life. There's one thing you'd better learn about me right now," he said, his eyes narrowing. "I don't tolerate lying." *Not from anyone. Not after what my ex-wife Liz did to me.*

She gave a funny little nod and looked away.

He wondered why, but then reminded himself not every woman had ulterior motives for everything they did. Not every woman could cold-heartedly do what Liz had done. The woman he thought he'd loved more than life itself had made a career out of lying. He gritted his teeth and pushed the vision of her hateful, but beautiful face to the back of his mind. It was time to move forward, not back. "Come on in," he repeated.

Hesitating, Ginger perched on the edge of the pool across from him, her slender legs dangling in the churning bubbles. Slowly, inch by tantalizing inch, she submerged her body, the water lapping at every luscious curve. When all of her skin from the neck down was hidden from his view, she closed her eyes. Resting her head against the tub she sighed through parted lips. "Ah, this is heaven."

Vince thought it was more like hell. His blood flowed hotter than the water he sat in. He smiled a wicked smile.

Why was it that whenever someone wanted something, but couldn't have it, the desire to possess it multiplied ten-fold? With the single-minded idea of acquiring what she so obviously deemed hands-off, Vince moved into her territory. Playing the predator she saw him as, he sat next to her. Not so close as to pose a threat, but close enough to touch her if invited. Or even if not. And God knew, he wanted to touch her.

"Are your muscles sore?" he asked, trailing his index finger along the silky trail of her arm.

Ginger's eyes shot open, surprise at his nearness evident in the wide stare of her blue eyes. She looked frightened, as if teetering on the edge of a precipice where one false move would send her reeling over.

Vince felt an unfamiliar need to wrap his arms around Ginger and protect her. It was ludicrous because he'd be protecting her from himself. His own conflicting emotions were tearing him apart. One part of him said to take it slow and easy. She was different than all the rest. Another part, the uncaged animal in him, wanted to take her where she sat.

The battle between desire and decency raged within him. With his breath erratic and his body stirring to life below the waist, he would be the first to admit it was an unsafe bet as to which side might win.

"I am a little sore," she admitted rubbing her neck with slender fingers.

On impulse, Vince reached over and placed his hands on Ginger's shoulders. When she jumped, he smiled. He had never met a woman as nervous as her. But she felt so good. So warm. So smooth. Vince couldn't have kept his hands from touching her if the building had been burning down around them. "Turn around," he urged, "I'll give you a massage."

She hesitated, flashed him another of her frightened doe looks, then turned her back toward him.

With sensuous skill, he kneaded her sore muscles. The water warmed her slick skin, heightening his awareness of her more than he thought humanly possible. She held herself rigid at first, then relaxed as his fingers worked magic. From his location behind her, he could see the mounds of her breasts, the darkened areolas showing through her tantalizing, barely there suit.

Shameless need, already taut as a rubberband, stretched to the breaking point. Vince groaned. Desire rapidly gained the advantage. Unable to stop himself, he lowered his head and placed his lips on Ginger's neck.

She flinched, but tilted her head to allow him better access.

His mouth wandered up and down the silky wet skin of her jaw line. As he nibbled on Ginger's ear, he slipped his arms below the water line and wrapped them around her slim waist. God, how long had it been? Kissing wasn't enough. He wanted to feel her beneath him, hear her moan his name in ecstasy, and bring her to the heights of passion.

As if reading his mind, she turned in his arms, placed her quivering palms flat against his chest. Her breathing was ragged, the apprehension evident in the nervous shift of her gaze. But she held him tight. When her lips parted slightly, it was the only invitation Vince needed.

With his blood pounding in his ears, he pulled her onto his lap and crushed her slick body to him. His lips ground against hers. He tasted a hint of chlorine on her lush mouth.

She matched his intensity, wrapping her arms about his neck and running her hands through his damp hair.

He had vowed earlier to make her admit she desired him. Though no words were spoken, there was no denying she ached for him as much as he wanted her. The evidence was in her lips, her fingertips, her wet body pressing against his arousal.

In the back of his mind good and evil readied for battle.

Don't do this, Vince. The woman deserves better than being taken in a public hot tub.

God, help me, but I can't stop.

Spanning her waist with his hands, he lifted her out of the water and set her on the edge, never breaking contact with lips or skin. "Water's too damn hot," he muttered against her succulent mouth.

Vince prayed he'd remembered to lock the door, because in about two seconds they would both be as naked as Adam and Eve. With his hand against her back and lowering her to the ground, he followed her out of the tub in one fluid move. Covering her like a blanket, he looked into her innocent blue eyes. He saw desire, heat, but also uncertainty.

A muscle ticked in his jaw. If he was a gentleman, he'd quit now, before he couldn't.

He knew only that he had to keep kissing her.

The knock on the door echoed around the small room. "Who's in there? Unlock this door right now."

"Shit," Vince swore under his breath. He placed his forehead against Ginger's for a second while he willed his racing heart to slow down. Great timing. Why did this have to happen now? It was obvious the day manager hadn't informed the night manager of their arrangement. He hadn't kidded Ginger when he'd told her he'd paid people to stay away. The supervisor had lit up like a neon sign at the amount of money that had passed hands for the "Out of Order" sign Vince had hung on the door on his way in.

With reluctance, he dragged himself off Ginger's warm body. A woman had not affected his head and his heart this way in a long time. Vince wasn't so sure he liked it. "Grab your stuff," he growled without looking at her. He couldn't bring himself to see what he'd almost possessed. Not if he wanted to keep his sanity. "We're leaving."

The struggle for victory between body and mind had ended. The choice had been taken from him. The battle was over. But the war was far from ended.

Instead of feeling glad, an overwhelming sense of frustration threatened to eat him alive.

After one very cold shower, Ginger lay on her mattress half listening to the T.V. news. Thoughts of Vince danced in her head and the frigid water had done nothing to alleviate them. She still felt his hard body pressed against hers, still saw the passion burning deep in his green eyes. A sense of longing and of loss coiled in the pit of her stomach.

Fidgeting, she punched the pillow behind her head. Ginger couldn't understand Vince's attitude. After telling the manager the door must have locked by accident, they rode up to their rooms in an uncomfortable silence. With a gruff goodbye that left her feeling miserable, he left her at her door, refusing to look her in the eye. Did he regret what had happened? Did she?

She should have a guilty conscience. Seeing what her mother had endured, being forced to raise a child by herself, she should know better than to be anybody's weekend fling. Following her mother's advice hadn't been a problem before. Why was she finding it so difficult now? A knock on the door interrupted her tortured thoughts.

Robyn scooted off her bed where she sat painting her toenails in a drop-dead shade of red. "It's about time room service got here. I'm starving." She walked across the room on her heels so her polish wouldn't smudge.

Ginger watched her go. With a black and white silk nightie, and her awkward stroll, Robyn resembled a penguin more than a full-grown woman. Ginger's lips twitched into the first real smile she'd felt in hours.

"Wow!" Robyn came back into the room with a long white box cradled in one arm.

"Did Rick send you flowers?" They certainly couldn't be for her. Vince had made it clear he didn't want to be around her.

Robyn's gaze grew wistful. "They're not for me."

Ginger's heart skipped a beat. They couldn't be from Vince. She flew off the bed with the grace of a badger and grabbed the box out of Robyn's hands. Carefully taking off the lid, she peeked inside. Peeling back the green tissue paper, she saw two dozen peach long-stemmed roses. Her breath caught in her throat and she reached for the note with an unsteady hand.

Vince's strong, masculine scrawl lined the card, his message simple and direct.

Sorry for being such a selfish animal. Meet me for dinner at eight . . . please? Vince.

"Robyn," she said, heading for the closet. "What have you got that I can wear?"

"Shall we? The limousine is waiting," Vince placed Ginger's hand in the crook of his elbow.

Standing so close to him, touching him, was more than she could take. Breathless, her insides quivering, she knew she was falling for him too hard and too fast. But there was absolutely nothing she could do to stop the riotous emotions flooding her body.

The massive muscles in his arm flexed beneath her hand as he reached for the door. No man has a right to look as handsome as he does, she reflected, taking in his black tuxedo. His hair, brushing against the top of his collar, shone as dark as the suit he wore. Ginger remembered how soft it was and longed to run her fingers through the thickness again.

She smoothed the palm of her free hand over the velvet of her black dress. The garment fit like a glove from the bodice to the skirt to the tight, full-length sleeves. The dress stopped at mid-thigh, exposing more leg than it probably should have.

"Don't do anything I wouldn't do," Robyn advised with a twinkle in her eyes as the pair headed out of the room.

Vince flashed a rakish grin.

Ginger frowned.

In the back of the limo, he kept a proper distance, staying on his side of the car. Disappointment shrouded Ginger like a heavy cloak, confirming in her mind the fact he regretted what had transpired between them earlier. Was he just trying to be nice? What did he want from her? Ginger glanced at his rugged profile. What did she want from him?

At the restaurant, he took the seat across from her. Candlelight twinkled on the table between them. Ginger leaned back in her chair and flashed an uneasy smile his way. The tension filtering through the air was as tangible as his leg brushing against hers.

He smiled back, but his face turned serious. "We need to talk."

Her heart plummeted like an elevator free of its cable. This was it. This was where he informed her it had been fun . . . but. She sighed. It was just as well.

Taking a deep breath, Ginger filled her lungs, then slowly expelled the air through parted lips. She lifted her gaze and stared across the table into the depths of his green eyes. She was ready. For whatever it was worth, he could dish out the worst and she could take it.

"I'm sorry for what happened earlier."

Her heart thumped audibly. Was he sorry it had happened or sorry for the interruption?

"I acted like an animal. You didn't deserve it."

No, but if Ginger had to be honest, she sure wanted it.

"I'm sure you get more than your fair share of unwanted attention. There's more to you than just a beautiful face and a knock-out body. You shouldn't have to put up with any man pawing you." He smiled, but the seriousness remained in his eyes.

Uncomfortable, Ginger tore her gaze from his searching eyes and studied the lace tablecloth. He'd stated earlier he hated liars.

Was it time to fess up, before it was too late? "There's something I need to tell you."

"No."

Her gaze skittered to his. "No?"

Vince's warm, large hand covered hers where it lay on top of the table. Her heart skipped a beat as she remembered their earlier intimacy. Heat filled her cheeks. She knew she was asking for trouble, but she couldn't help it. She wanted to feel his warm touch on her again.

The candlelight danced in his eyes, lending him a devilish quality that proved irresistible. "I want you and you want me," he whispered. "But I refuse to take advantage of you. I'm leaving tomorrow afternoon. Until that time, you and I are going to enjoy each other's company. Nothing less, nothing more. No revelations . . . no surprises. Unless," he smiled, "you have a husband hidden away somewhere?"

Ginger shook her head. "No husband. Just an ex-fiancé."

"Ex? What happened?" he questioned.

Her gaze locked with his. "I guess my heart knew you were coming." The words spilled out before she could stop them. Spontaneity wasn't normal for her. Carefully measuring her words before she spoke had kept her out of a lot of unwanted trouble. Today she had strayed from her own self-imposed code of conduct. Not once, but several times, she reminded herself.

Vince's eyes danced with more than just the light from the table. "Do you remember when I asked you if you believed in fate last night?"

She nodded. Was it only last night? It felt like she'd known this man for ages.

"Do you believe in it now?" he asked.

Ginger picked up her crystal wine glass, pretending to study the swirling red liquid. "You could persuade me." Persuade? What a laugh. All he had to do was lead the way and she'd be right behind him like a kid playing follow the leader.

"Tell me about yourself," she asked, wanting to change the subject before she revealed her emotions. The waiter placed their heated platters before them.

Vince picked up a knife and dug into his juicy steak. "What do you want to know?"

Ginger propped her chin on her palm and watched him enjoy his food. "What do you like to do when you're not working?"

"Well, when I have time I'm a big brother to underprivileged kids."

Ginger knew then her mother was dead wrong. Any man that bothered to look after other people's children couldn't ever walk away from his own. At least not this man. She already knew he had patience from their day spent on the slopes. Now she knew he cared about people.

In the limousine heading back to the hotel, Vince linked his fingers with hers and they rode in a companionable silence the entire way. It was late when they strode across the hotel's marble foyer. An odd assortment of partyers filled the lounge, their laughter echoing throughout the lobby.

With a quiet swish of the elevator doors, all sounds faded. Ginger stood next to Vince, arms touching, fingers locked. Neither said anything. They both watched the light change from floor to floor as if it were the most fascinating contraption ever invented.

A bell indicated they'd reached their destination. In studied silence, they walked to Ginger's room. Anticipation threatened to cut off her breathing. Would they resume what they had started earlier at the hot tub? Part of her wanted to. Another part feared they would.

Her need for Vince scared her. Letting herself open to any kind of emotion was leaving her exposed to the same kind of pain her mother had faced. She wasn't sure she was ready.

At her door, he took her by the shoulders and turned her around to face him. Ginger took a deep breath

He didn't kiss her, but pulled her into his arms instead. Ginger rested her chin on his shoulder and wrapped her arms around his waist. She could stay here for eternity, holding him. She closed her eyes and moved her face into the crook of his neck savoring the musky smell of his cologne, the warmth of his embrace. A sigh escaped her lips.

"Tired?" he asked.

"Content," she said. As soon as she said the words, a strange sense of foreboding washed over her. Something didn't feel right. Ginger's eyes snapped open. At the dark end of the hallway, a man stood staring from the shadows. She gasped as he turned and fled around a corner.

"What's wrong?" Vince demanded, grabbing her by the shoulders.

"Th-there's a man watching us," she said, pointing in the direction he went.

"Stay here," he insisted, striding away.

Ginger grabbed his sleeve. A shiver of terror ran through her. "Are you crazy? I'm not staying here by myself." She followed quickly, dogging his every step.

They turned the corner to find the hallway empty. "Are you sure someone was there?"

She could see the doubt in his eyes. "Of course." Her indignant tone raised one of his eyebrows. "I think he's been following me since yesterday."

"Why would anyone be following you? Could he have seen you modeling or something?"

Headlines of women murdered by crazed stalkers danced in her head, and she rubbed her hands over her arms trying to get rid of the goosebumps. This couldn't be happening to her. She wasn't even a real model. "Oh, God, I have no clue. I haven't done anything. Why would anyone be following me? I don't like it. This is too creepy."

Vince draped a supporting arm around her shoulder. She wanted to curl into the safety of his arms and stay there forever. At his warm touch, the fear slowly vanished.

Once again at Ginger's door, Vince held his hand out for her key. Opening the lock, he pushed the door open and pulled her into his arms. As his lips descended to Ginger's, she closed her eyes for a searing kiss that blazed a trail all the way to her toes.

"Do you want another lesson tomorrow morning?"

"Yes," she whispered, relishing the feel of

his arms about her, dreaming of what would come next.

He kissed the tip of her nose. "I meant a skiing lesson."

Ginger had the grace to color, but shamelessly clung to him anyway.

With a tender touch, he unclenched her hands. "I refuse to take advantage of you, remember?"

"Yeah. I remember." How was she supposed to forget? A heavy weight settled in the pit of her stomach. "Meet you in the lobby at nine?"

"Fine." With a hand at the small of her back, he hastened her into the room. "Sleep tight," he said, closing the door between them.

"Sleep tight, my butt," Ginger mumbled for the tenth time, tossing and turning on the uncomfortable hotel mattress. Robyn's gentle snore in the other bed irritated her and she was half tempted to whip a pillow at Robyn's head just for spite. It wasn't fair that the rest of the world could sleep while all she could think of was Vince.

Vince smiling that damned devilish grin. Vince kissing her. Vince getting in his car and driving out of her life forever. She lay looking up at the shadows dancing on the ceiling. She couldn't let him leave without knowing how it felt to be with him . . . in every sense of the word. She smiled in the darkness as a plan formed in her mind.

"What are you doing up already?" Robyn leaned on one elbow and pushed a mass of tangled dark curls out of her eyes. "And where the hell did you get that?"

Ginger looked down at the flesh-colored silk teddy she wore, then up at her friend. Doubts plagued her. She forced them away with a shake of her head. "Close your mouth, Robyn. You'll catch flies."

Robyn pushed herself up onto her knees, shock evident in her wide stare. "You have two seconds to tell me what's going on. And don't spare any details. God, you look naked in that thing. Where did you get it, why did you keep it a secret, and can I borrow it sometime?"

Grabbing her red ski pants, Ginger pulled them on over the flimsy teddy, trying to hide her scanty outfit. Her hands shook with apprehension, but nothing could stop her now that her mind was made up. "I had the manager open the gift shop early for me. I told him it was a matter of life or death." She cringed remembering the man's look of skepticism while she paid for her purchase.

71

It wasn't like her to do any of this. She had to prove to herself her mother was wrong. Ginger wanted to have a relationship with a man, even if only for the weekend, and survive. Was she only kidding herself?

"You're going to catch pneumonia skiing with only underwear on beneath your ski outfit."

"I don't plan on skiing today."

"Oh, my God." The brunette's hands flew to her mouth. She got off the bed and stood in front of Ginger, tears evident in her eyes. "I have never been so proud in all my life."

Standing in front of the door to the penthouse suite, Ginger wondered if she was doing the right thing. There was nothing vile or contemptible about wanting to spend time with Vince. Even if she'd only known him two short days, that didn't make her a woman of loose morals.

It was, in all honesty, a matter of one heart seeking another. One human searching for someone to care about. And she did care for Vince. If she had more time to get to know him, he could easily steal the key to her heart.

The tightness in Ginger's chest told her what she didn't really want to hear. She couldn't deny the deep feelings that attracted her to Vince. She wanted more than one weekend with him, but if one weekend was all he could give, she'd take it and run.

With a conviction as strong as iron, she knocked on the door.

Chapter 4

His tan body contrasted sharply with her pale, creamy skin. As soft as a whisper, he ran one of his hands down the hollow of her throat, between her generous breasts, down the flat of her stomach, to the juncture of her thighs.

She was naked.

Gloriously naked.

Her golden hair spilled like a waterfall over the white silk sheets.

She moaned as his fingers slipped inside her tight sheath. "Oh, Vince," she gasped, her hips thrusting against his touch. "Take me now. I need you now."

Vince looked down at himself to discover he was already naked. When had that happened? It didn't matter. He was ready to fulfill her every fantasy. Clothes would only slow things down, anyway. He straddled her, and spread her thighs apart with one hand.

A persistent knocking on the door finally woke him up. "Dammit!" Vince swore with a vicious kick to the twisted covers. "Never fails," he muttered, realizing it was just a dream. Rubbing a hand over his face, he grabbed the sheet off the bed and wrapped it around his waist.

Striding across the plush carpet in bare feet, he reached the door and yanked it open, ready to reprimand the bastard who dared interrupt his dreams. The woman of his fantasy stood on the threshold.

He clutched the white satin sheet tighter, trying to hide his morning arousal, and ran a hand through his hair. "God, did I oversleep?" He looked at his wrist, realizing he'd left his watch on the nightstand.

"No. I'm early. Can I come in?"

Vince stepped aside. "Of course." Alarm bells went off in his head as he took in her pale face and her eyes darting everywhere but at him. An unexplainable fear gripped his heart. "Is something wrong?"

"No . . . I . . ."

"What is it, Ginger? What do you want? Has something happened?" With a finger under the soft skin of her chin, he forced her to look him in the eye.

She hesitated, shifting from one foot to the other nervously. "I want you to take advantage of me," she announced without blinking. Her eyes held his, the strength of her convictions, the burning desire evident in her stare.

Vince couldn't have been more surprised if a bomb had exploded in the expensive living room of the penthouse suite. He closed his eyes and swallowed. Normally, he took whatever a woman offered. But Ginger wasn't anything like Liz or any of the other females he preferred to date. Not even close. She deserved more than he could ever hope to give.

He couldn't just take her for a quick romp in the hay and then cast her aside. Even if she said she wanted him to. And Lord, hadn't she just said those very words?

If he slept with her, he'd have to keep her. Sweat formed on his palms. He didn't know if he was ready for that type of commitment. He had to put distance between them. "Let me get dressed," he said, running a shaky hand through his sleep-tousled hair. "I'll be right back." Vince donned a pair of Levi's and shrugged on a denim shirt, not bothering to button it.

When he returned to the living room, Ginger stood exactly where he'd left her, misery etched in every line of her face. He felt like the biggest heel on earth. He didn't want to cause her pain. He didn't want to reject her, but it seemed no matter what course he took, she was going to be hurt.

Was she even aware of the consequences? Did she even care?

"Do you mind if I take my coat off? It's getting hot in here," Ginger asked.

Good. Changing the subject was good. Maybe they could avoid the whole issue of sleeping together. "You might as well. I'm going to order room service before we hit the slopes anyway." With his back to Ginger, he reached for the phone and dialed. At the sound of her softly muttered oaths, he turned around.

Ginger struggled with her zipper. With a jerk of her fingers, the teeth unsnagged. The red parka slipped off Ginger's shoulders revealing her skimpy underwear and miles and miles of creamy, bare skin.

Shock shot through him with the force of a hurricane. "What the hell?" The phone slipped from his hand forgotten. "Put your jacket back on right now!" he sputtered. The item she wore covered more of her body than the bikini she'd had on last night, but because of its color, which blended with her own skin tone, she looked nude. And Vince's body responded with a primal urge he had no hope of ever controlling. Heat coiled through him like a fire fueled with gasoline. His heart hammered in his chest. He hardened against his will.

"Make me," she demanded in a husky whisper, her eyes smoldering.

He knew if he touched Ginger there would be no going back. He closed his eyes and counted to ten. "Behave, Ginger," he said through clenched teeth, a muscle in his neck pulsing out of control.

"I'm tired of behaving."

At the sound of another zipper his eyes flew open.

The woman was actually removing her ski pants! Dropping the red material to the floor, she advanced seductively towards him, all legs. Longer legs than God should have allowed one woman to possess.

Vince moved backward trying to keep space between them for the sake of sanity. The hard wall met his back. He was forced to stand still. She kept moving and stopped with nothing but inches between them. Her warm, delicate hands slid up his bare chest, sending shock waves of lust throughout his body.

Vince cursed himself for not having taken the time to button his shirt. His breathing accelerated to an erratic level. His mind struggled to find a reason why he shouldn't grab her and make wild and passionate love to her.

He threw his hands up in the air, refusing

to touch her, using every ounce of the self-control he possessed to avoid physical contact. God, but her soft hands on his body felt good. "I don't want to hurt you, Ginger," he said in a voice hoarse with ragged emotion.

"I'm not asking you to hurt me. I'm asking you . . . begging you . . . to make love to me." She punctuated her words by placing tiny kisses up and down his bare chest.

The scent of her perfume wafted to his nostrils, invading the chink in his willpower. "Same thing." He kept his gaze leveled on the ceiling. Looking at her would be too much of a temptation.

"I'm not trying to wring a commitment out of you." Ginger placed her hands on his cheeks and forced him to look at her. "I just want something to remember you by. It's as simple as that. Is it asking too much?"

"Yes!" Forgetting his resolve not to touch her, Vince grabbed her by the shoulders and looked into the depths of her ocean-blue eyes. Was the woman crazy? She may not be asking for a commitment, but if he slept with her, he'd have to give her one. "Don't you understand? It's *not* as simple as that. Nothing is ever as simple as that!"

He felt her stiffen beneath his grip. Her eyes turned into cold chips of ice. "Fine, I can take a hint. If you don't want me I'll leave." She tried to pull free.

He wouldn't let her. God, was she deliberately misunderstanding him? Hadn't he shown her since the minute they met how much he wanted her? What did she need . . . a neon sign declaring the need he felt? "Don't want you? Lady, you can't begin to imagine how very much I *do* want you." Throwing aside caution, determined to show her what words couldn't begin to reveal, he crushed her silk-encased body to his naked chest. "Oh, God. I can't fight this anymore. I'm only human. Too human." He groaned, his lips possessing hers with a hunger he couldn't contain.

He'd known if he touched her he wouldn't be able to stop. He'd been right.

Their kisses turned hot and feverish, as if they both wanted, needed to make up for lost time. Vince ran his hands up and down the small of her back while Ginger's long slender fingers blazed a trail across his chest in a touch as soft as a butterfly. He all but drowned in the warm sensation flooding his body.

When her tongue slipped across his upper lip, Vince captured it in his mouth drawing it in to dance with his. He moved his exploration to her throat. "You feel so good," he murmured, her velvety, soft hair brushing against his cheek, the innocent touch exciting him even further.

She answered with little whimpers as she ran her fingers through his dark locks. Tingles radiated through every nerve-ending he possessed.

"God, I need you, Ginger." With one finger, Vince slipped the spaghetti strap off her shoulder and peeled down the flesh-colored teddy to expose one breast. Lifting the generous mound with his hand, he took the extended pink nipple into his mouth, circling the nub with his tongue, teasing it with gentle tugs between his teeth.

Her whimpers turned to moans that drove him wild. "We should take it slow," he breathed against her skin.

"Why?" she sighed, rubbing her hand along the hard bulge in his jeans.

All traces of reason fled. He couldn't think with her in his arms, her body against his. "Beats me." His mouth sought hers again, his hand brushing against the juncture of her legs. She slid his zipper open, and he closed his eyes and groaned when Ginger gently stroked his rock-hard length.

It was the most wonderful, and the most torturous sensation he'd ever experienced. He was coming unglued like never before.

"I'm not going to make it to the bed," he gritted out, his face pressed between the hollow of her breasts. She smelled just washed, fresh out of the shower, and he breathed in her scent.

"Beds are overrated."

A smile flitted across his face. Where had this woman been all his life? He'd never felt this alive, this needed. Vince sank to his knees and pulled her with him, slipping the other strap from her bare shoulder. His eyes never leaving hers, he pulled the garment to her waist.

Desire, hot and untempered, flickered in her eyes.

Vince licked lips as dry as the desert. He had felt the fasteners of her teddy moments earlier, and skillfully unsnapped them with one flick of his finger and one twist of his wrist.

Her eyes widened, then closed as his fingers slipped inside her warm, inviting sheath. Ginger's head fell back languidly. Vince took the opportunity to slide his tongue along the delicate arch of her neck while his fingers stroked in and out.

A rush of breath escaped her lips against his ear and her fingernails made little welts on his upper arms. Her hips moved in rhythm with him.

"If I didn't know better I'd say you liked this even better than skiing." He lifted his head in time to see a smile tug at her lips, as she gave a deep, breathy sigh to confirm his statement.

Ginger leaned into him, sliding her body against his erection and tugging his jeans down his hips. Vince withdrew his fingers from her warmth to help. Free of any encumbrances, he knelt before her, proud and stiff, ready and more than a little willing.

Pulling her to his naked body, he caressed her lovingly trying to hold back the need building inside him. Ginger took his hand and kissed the inside of his wrist. The sensation ripped a moan from his throat. How could one simple touch from a woman affect him so? Keeping his hand in hers, she laid back on the carpet and pulled him eagerly to her.

He slid his body along the length of hers, reveling in the feel of her satiny skin against his. No woman had ever inundated him with such helpless pleasure. God, what had she done to him? Better yet, why didn't he care that he was mindlessly under her spell?

Like a hungry man devouring his last meal, Vince attacked her lips. She matched his assault with one of her own, wildly kneading the firm flesh of his buttocks.

Ready to explode, he parted her legs with his knee. She opened easily for him and wrapped her legs around his waist like she'd never let go.

He didn't want her to.

With a shaky hand, Vince guided himself into the silken warmth between her legs. She wanted him. The realization flowed over him like warm honey, and he realized that he wanted her. No — not just wanted her — coveted her with an intensity that shook him to the core. He held himself up with his hands on either side of her face while he kissed her lips. He pushed himself into her sweet center as far as he could go.

She was tight and slick and hot.

Everything he needed.

Everything he desired.

His eyes half closed in passion and heady pleasure. Her hands slid up his chest and wrapped around his neck, dragging his lips back to hers. Her breath was warm against his mouth as she spoke. "Vince, oh God, Vince. Why did we wait so long? Oh, God," she whimpered. "Faster. I need . . . Vince . . . please . . . oh God, yes . . . harder."

Vince pulled out and pushed in again and again, building in tempo along with Ginger's undulating hips. Together they rode the storm of their passion.

Sweat trickled down his back. The strength of his climax took him unaware. His mind and body spiraled out of control and then exploded in bursts of exquisite pleasure. He called out her name, then felt Ginger reach her own peak, her body contracting around him. Her fingers gripped his biceps, her whole body tensing.

They clung together in a blissful afterglow. Finally spent, Vince rolled onto his back and pulled her into the circle of his embrace.

They lay silent for a long moment, each trying to capture their breath. "I just have one question," Ginger said, trailing a finger from his bottom lip down his chin.

"What?" God, she was beautiful with her hair a disheveled mess about her face. She looked like she'd just been loved, and Vince was damn glad he'd been the one to do it.

"Is it always like this for you? I mean . . . wow." Wonder filtered through her whispered voice.

Vince knew exactly what she meant. He'd made love to a lot of women, but never had he experienced such unchecked passion. "No. It's never been like this. You make me feel like a sex-starved teenager. You make love like you ski . . . totally out of control." He hardened again just thinking about

being inside her. "Lady, I've never met anyone like you in my life." He rolled over and
pinned her luscious naked body to the
carpet.

Her blue eyes widened, then a smile
spread across her face. When her hand
found him, he closed his eyes and sighed
with the pleasure of it. "You keep this up,
lady, and I'll have to get rough." Vince
punctured his words with tiny gentle kisses
on her lips, down her neck and around her
breasts.

"I think," she whispered, her hand gently
stroking, "that I m gonna like it rough."

Ginger threw her hands above her head
and stretched the kinks out of her tired
body. After hours of lovemaking, they had
finally managed to make it to the silk-lined
sheets of the bed. She looked at Vince lying
next to her. One pitch-black lock of his hair
curled across his forehead. She longed to
touch it, but kept her hand at her side.

A lump formed in her throat and Ginger
swallowed it down. She would miss him.
She'd never forget this day, this time with
him. She would treasure it forever. Tears
formed in her eyes and she blinked them
back.

"Why are you crying?"

Startled, Ginger's gaze flew to his. God, he was supposed to be asleep. He wasn't supposed to see her crying. Why hadn't she fought her emotions until she was alone? She had foolishly told herself she'd only wanted something to remember him by. Well, she'd got what she wanted. So why, now that it was almost over, almost time for him to go, did she feel so miserable?

His hand reached up and wiped away an errant tear.

Turning her head, she kissed his palm. "Thanks for the memories," she whispered.

Leaning on one elbow, his supple, masculine form towered over her, his green eyes filled with anger. "Get it straight right now. This isn't only for today, Cooper. We're going to love our whole lives through."

More tears sprang to her eyes and overflowed, running down her cheeks. "What?" Her pounding heart threatened to break free from her chest. A nervous laugh escaped her lips. "I . . . you . . . we . . . what?" *Oh, God, I'm a babbling idiot.*

Vince laughed, a rich baritone sound that was music to her ears. "Why do women always cry when they're happy?"

She still refused to believe what she thought she'd heard. Leaning on her elbow, she looked him directly in the eyes. She had to know — had to be sure she understood what he meant. "Am I happy?"

"Hell yes, you are."

"Why am I happy?" she asked on a breathless whisper.

Vince leaned over and kissed the corner of her mouth. "Because, with your permission, of course, we're going to see where this relationship can take us. I'm not moving to Denver for two more weeks, but I'd like to call you — every night. I'd like to spend Christmas with you. I'd like to make love to you until I'm too old to get it up anymore."

Every emotion Ginger had ever experienced in her life tried to fight its way out at the same time. She wanted to cry, she wanted to laugh, she wanted to hit him for making her think earlier the only thing he wanted was a one-night stand. Instead she pushed him down on the bed and straddled his perfect body with her own.

With no resistance from him, she pinned his arms above his head and leaned down close, so close her breasts rubbed against his chest. "Buster, we've just spent seven hours making love. I don't think the words 'can't get it up' are even in your vocabulary."

His eyes widened. "Seven hours? Christ, what time is it?" His gaze snapped to the clock on the bedside table, and his head fell back on the pillow. "Oh, my God, it's two o'clock."

Puzzled, Ginger asked, "Why. What happens at two? Do you turn into a pumpkin?" She wiggled her body against his, the juncture of her thighs pressing against his erection, trying to make him forget time and the rest of the world.

Vince squeezed her breasts in answer, then picked her up by the waist and physically moved her off him. "I have a limo coming in half an hour. I have a plane to catch. Sorry, angel." He got off the bed and started searching for his clothes.

This was it. The beginning of the end. She could feel it in the knot in the pit of her stomach. He really was leaving. Ginger closed her eyes and tried to quell the angry storm of tears. She'd fought any kind of emotion for so long she didn't know how to handle them anymore. The bed sagged on one side and Ginger's eyes opened as Vince wrapped his arms around her.

"I'm a man of my word, Ginger. I never lie." He kissed her temple and brushed a lock of hair out of her eyes. "I *will* call you every night, I promise. Hell, lady, if it's any consolation, I need you so much it scares the daylights out of me."

The warmth of his chest comforted her as

she pressed her cheek against it and hugged him tight in the middle of the king-sized bed. "I'm afraid," she admitted.

"I'll be with you the entire way. We'll tackle this ride together." He kissed the top of her head and pulled her closer. "Now get that sexy body of yours into some clothes before you make me miss my ride." He playfully smacked her bare rump.

When Ginger finally had her red ski parka back on, Vince walked her back to her room. They stood on the threshold of the open door. Ginger had never felt so confused in her entire life. Happiness threatened to overwhelm her, but sadness from their forced separation followed close on its tail.

"Is your phone number in the book?"

"Yes. I mean no!" She was listed under her real name, Ginger Thompson, not Ginger Cooper. "I'm unlisted." She crossed her fingers behind her back to unjinx the little white lie. She'd explain the truth when they saw each other again in two weeks. They'd both have a big laugh over it, she was sure. "Let me write it down on a piece of paper for you."

Entering the room, she heard the shower running in the bathroom. Robyn must have finished skiing for the day. Ginger scoured the place for a pen. Hotels always had complimentary pens lying around. Why couldn't she find one when she needed it? It didn't help that Vince dogged her every step, wrapping his arms about her waist every time she stopped to search in a drawer.

"You're not helping," she accused when he stuck his tongue in her ear and wicked sensations spiraled throughout her body. "Robyn is going to finish her shower and come walking out of the bathroom naked."

"That would be embarrassing."

"More for us than her, trust me." She spied Robyn's purse on the dresser. If an object couldn't be found in that woman's bag, chances were, it didn't exist. She fished her hand in and dug out a silver pen while Vince's mouth worked a trail from her ear down her neck to the front of her parka. His white teeth tugged on the tip of her breast through the thick red material. Grabbing a note pad, Ginger wrote down her number and squirming loose from his grip, turned and handed it to Vince. "Here. Don't lose it."

He glanced at the paper, then folded it carefully and tucked it into his wallet. "Not on your life." His strong arms reached out and pulled her back into his arms. Their lips met in a final kiss that exploded in every nerve ending Ginger possessed. She clutched his shirt and stood on tiptoes, never wanting the kiss to end.

Vince pulled away, regret flashing in his eyes. "That's to keep you warm until we meet again. I'll call you tomorrow night." With flick of his finger on the end of her nose, he turned and walked out of the room. Looking back, he winked as the door closed behind him.

"Oh, God," Ginger whispered as she placed shaking fingers to her burning lips. "Is this what it feels like to fall head-over-heels in love?"

Chapter 5

"I've met someone special, Mom." Ginger stabbed a bite of salad with a fork and peered at the woman across from her under the covered veil of her lashes.

"Oh?"

It was amazing how her mother could pack so much meaning into one two-letter word. There was no mistaking the tightening of the older woman's lips, the straightening of her back, the glazed, knowing look in her eyes. Eva Thompson wasn't pleased.

Ginger took a deep breath and forged ahead anyway, knowing her idea would go over like a clown at a funeral. "I like him. I feel confident he likes me, too. He's asked to spend Christmas with us."

Laying her silverware neatly at the side of her plate, Ginger's mom tucked a lock of silver hair behind one ear then folded her hands in her lap. "Do you really think that's wise? What do you know about him? What does he do for a living? What are his parents like? For that matter, what's *he* like?"

Why, Mom, he's everything you despise. He's sexy and virile and more man than a woman could ever handle. He's so good-looking I could literally stare at him all day. Oh, and by the way, he's dangerous. One look at him and I forget all the advice you've ever given me. I'm totally helpless. And I love it. Inundated with questions, Ginger could only answer, "He's very nice. You'll like him." *Yeah, right. Dream on, Gin. Your mother only likes men if they're half dead and could in no way, shape, or form, intentionally or unintentionally, attempt to destroy a woman's hopes and dreams.*

"Well, I just feel holidays are for family."

Ginger put her fork down since her appetite had vanished. *Families have to grow. Why won't you let ours?* "What if he wants to become a part of our family?"

Eva's blue eyes widened in surprise. Festive music over the restaurant speaker filled the silence. Leaning forward, she scanned the lunch crowd at nearby tables as if to make sure they weren't eavesdropping. "Has he asked you to marry him?" she quizzed, leaning closer across the table so her whispered words weren't lost.

Ginger knew this was coming. "Not in those exact words, no." She fidgeted in her chair, like a schoolgirl caught in a lie. She wasn't as sure about her relationship with Vince as she had been five minutes earlier.

That's what mothers were for, wasn't it? To make one feel insecure, awkward, ten years old again. She knew Vince wanted her, not just for her body, a quick one-nighter, but for *her.* But it'd been two days without so much as a message from him. He'd promised he was a man of his word.

Ginger chastised herself. She couldn't let her mother's negativity get to her. Nothing was wrong. It was only two short days. He was a businessman. He was probably busy doing business things. He'd call when he could.

"Oh, honey," her mother clicked her tongue and shot Ginger an I-told-you-so look. "How many times do we have to go over this? If a man doesn't ask for any type of commitment, he only wants one thing. Did you sleep with him?"

"Mother!" How could she answer *that* question? *Yes, Mom. I did. And I'd do it again in a heartbeat.*

"I'm just trying to protect you. I just don't want you to get hurt the way I've been hurt. I've told you before that a sexy man is a dan—"

Ginger rolled her eyes. How could she forget something that was carved in her brain like words on a tombstone? "I know, I know. A sexy man is a dangerous man. Vince isn't like that. Although I'll admit he's extremely handsome, he's also very reliable."

"Are you sure about this? You haven't known him very long, have you?"

She spoke with as much conviction as she could muster.

"Intuition."

"A woman," Eva informed her, "can't rely on intuition where a man is involved. Men tend to muddle the head. I know from experience you'll never hear from him again. You'd do well to forget him right now, Ginger. I think you should talk to Steven and try to iron things out with him." She hardened her voice as if she intended her words to sting. "If he'll have you back after you dumped him."

"Steven wasn't right for me, Mother." Ginger picked up her fork and stabbed at her salad again. She wasn't a little girl anymore, even if her mother made her feel like one. Clenching her hand so tight the fork bent in her grip, she clipped out, "Why should I settle for someone I know I'm not going to be happy with? Why? I could never be content with Steven. With Vince, I don't know — it feels so different." Comparing

Steven and Vince was like comparing dishwater with the finest champagne.

Eva laughed, a harsh sound that grated on Ginger's nerves. "No man is right for a woman. Who says that *different* is good? Steven was dependable. These days dependable is hard to come by. Different will end up getting you hurt." She waved her fork in Ginger's direction. "Mark my words."

"Well, maybe that's for me to decide. Maybe for once in my life I'd like to be able to feel some emotion. That's why you've never called my father, isn't it?" A lump formed in her throat when she thought of the man she'd never met, the wasted years she'd longed to know who he was. "You're afraid to feel. I don't want to end up a lonely, bitter woman like you." Ginger regretted her words as soon as she saw the crestfallen look on her mother's face.

Pushing her cane-backed chair away from the table, Eva grabbed her purse and stood. "I'm sorry I've been such a bad influence on you." Her lips pinched into a thin line. "I'm sorry I want nothing but the best for my little girl. I'll just go home and mind my own pathetic life instead of trying to make yours as miserable as mine." Turning, she wove her way around the tables.

"Mom, wait!" Too late. Eva Thompson was gone. Ginger knew it would take her a long time to get over this one. *God, how could I be so stupid?* She put her elbow on the table and plopped her forehead on her hand.

"Will you be wanting your check, miss?"

Ginger looked up at the smirking waiter. He'd obviously enjoyed the little tiff he'd witnessed. "Yes," she snapped.

Paying the bill, Ginger rushed out to her car and scrambled inside to evade the chill December wind. She thought long and hard about her mother's words on her way back to work. She certainly couldn't go back to Steven. Not now. Not ever. Steven was kind and considerate and boring. Vince was anything but boring. The man gave new meaning to the word "excitement." He gave new meaning to her life.

She marched through the doors of the Tyler Modeling Agency and to her reception desk with a purposeful stride that said "I know what I want and I'm going to get it."

"I had a weird call while you were gone, Gin," Tracy, her lunchtime replacement said. "A guy called asking if we had a model working here by the name of Ginger Cooper. He described her for me. I told him we had a receptionist that fit the bill, but your last name was different."

Ginger's heart leapt into her throat. Her breathing stopped, and her knees grew so weak she had to place a hand on the desk to support herself. "Did he give his name?" she asked on a breathless whisper. It had to be Vince. No one else would ask for a Ginger Cooper. Because Ginger Cooper didn't exist.

"No, but he sure sounded sexy," she said with a twinkle in her eye. "He insisted the woman he was looking for was beautiful, definitely a model. I told him that you were attractive, but he was adamant. Whoever this drop-dead gorgeous Ginger is, she's got the man wrapped around her little finger."

Tucking a stray hair behind her ear, Ginger pretended indifference by grabbing a stack of messages and shuffling through them while her heart beat so hard she was afraid it would burst out of her chest. "I'm sure it's just a coincidence." Wrapped around her finger? Vince?

"Yeah. Seemed weird at the time, though." Tracy grabbed her purse from a desk drawer. "I'm going to lunch. See you later."

"Okay." Lost in her thoughts, Ginger barely managed to wave. Why was Vince trying to track her down? She'd given him her home phone number. Why hadn't he used it? Nausea swept over her. Had he found out about her lie? The phone rang and her palms sweat when she reached for it. Was it Vince? Was he calling to say their relationship was over?

"Tyler Agency. May I help you?"

A rush of relief washed over her when a female responded. She transferred the call, but spent the rest of the afternoon a nervous wreck. Every time she picked up the phone she half-expected, half-feared the deep timbre of Vince's sexy voice on the other end of the line.

"Two weeks have already gone by. How long are you going to sit by that phone and wait for a call any fool would know isn't coming?" Robyn stood in front of Ginger, her hands on her hips in an authoritative manner.

"He'll call." How many times had Ginger told herself that since they'd returned? She plucked a lace-edged throw pillow off the sofa and hugged it to her chest. Every night she'd rushed home from work eagerly anticipating the sound of Vince's voice. And every night she'd gone to bed with tears in her eyes and her hopes becoming fainter with each day the awaited call failed to come. She still didn't understand how he'd tracked her down at the office. Something wasn't right. None of it made sense.

Robyn pleaded with her. "I know how much you care for him. For your sake, I hope he does call. But, Gin, you can't sit around the rest of your life waiting for him. You've got to get a move on."

"But what if —"

"You've got an answering machine."

The sympathy in her friend's eyes was unmistakable. *God, do I look as pathetic as I feel?* "I don't think I could go out in public just yet."

Robyn sat on the other end of the sofa, her legs tucked under her, and turned to face Ginger. "I wasn't going to ask you this, but I think it might be a perfect solution. It'll get you out of the house and away from that damn phone." She shot a nasty look at it.

"What is it?"

"Well, do you remember Rick, the guy I met up in Steamboat?"

"Of course." Ginger remembered the man made her uneasy, but Robyn seemed to really like him. After the argument she'd had with her mother, who was she to complain about anyone's choice of dating material?

"Well, he's booked a room at the Broadmoor in Colorado Springs. He wants to take me there tomorrow night."

"And you want me to come with you?"

"Not hardly," Robyn replied drolly, flashing Ginger a two's-company-three's-a-crowd look. "Again, I wouldn't ask this from you, but like I said, you're going to go crazy if you hang around here much longer. I need you to take my place cleaning the high-rise tomorrow. It's just for one evening. You don't have to see anyone, it will get you out of the house and you can dress as crummy as you want. What do you say? You'd really be doing me a favor."

Ginger saw the pleading look in Robyn's eyes. "You really like Rick, don't you?"

"More than I've liked anyone in a long time."

Yeah, and I like Vince more than I've liked anyone my whole life. "All right, for you, I'll do it." She smiled when she saw the relief spreading across her friend's face.

Robyn grabbed her purse off the coffee table and fished around inside. Her hand came back out with a key ring loaded with keys of various shapes and sizes. "Since you've done this for me before, I don't need to tell you anything. Oh, I just remembered. There's a new office moving in. The staff is already here, but the president of the company won't arrive until Monday. They take up the entire tenth floor. I haven't had the pleasure of meeting the guy yet, but the building manager says he can be very difficult. Just make sure it's spotless so we can make him happy. I guess he's been a real bear to work with." She grimaced.

Great, just what Ginger needed, a man with a bad temper. Of course, the way she felt right now, if some guy had the nerve to give her any lip, she'd probably take his head off. "He's not due until Monday though, right?"

"Right. You have nothing to worry about."

The next evening Ginger arrived at the office building dressed in baggy grey sweats with a red scarf tied around her unwashed hair, happy that vacuuming and emptying garbage cans didn't dictate a more elaborate wardrobe. The way she still felt, she didn't care what she looked like anyway.

After cleaning two floors with the help of Robyn's staff, Ginger moved to the tenth floor. Her friend had been wrong. Getting out of the house didn't get her mind off her problems. Vacuuming was brainless work that allowed the mind to wander at will. And wander it did. All over Vince. How he looked in his tight jeans; how he looked in his tuxedo; how he looked in his birthday suit. This was much worse than staying at home.

"Damn him," she muttered, turning off the vacuum and grabbing a rag from her cart. Viciously, she attacked the chrome drinking fountain by the elevators, rubbing it clean until it sparkled. Would she ever be free of the memory of him? God, she must be going crazy. Ginger could swear she even smelled his cologne.

An office door slammed and Ginger jumped. It was eerie to be in the huge building virtually alone. It conjured up sinister movie images and stories of ghosts. Her heart nearly stopped when she turned around and saw a man standing at the elevators with his back to her. Had she been so lost in her thoughts she hadn't been aware of anyone else's presence? That bordered on dangerous.

She stole another glance at the man. His dark hair hung over the back of his collar. It reminded her of Vince, except it was a tad longer. The fit of his suit reminded her of him also. If she didn't know better . . . Ginger's heart stopped beating. The rag in her hand fell to the ground.

With a ding, the elevator doors opened

and the man turned sideways, giving Ginger a view of his profile. A gasp escaped her lips. At the sound, he looked toward her. Ginger had the good sense to turn around and fumble with the objects on her cart.

It *was* Vince!

God help her, he was here, ten feet from her, and she couldn't even run to him. Never mind that she was dressed like a derelict. He didn't want her. The fact he'd never called told her that much. She hastily pushed her supplies around a corner and leaned against the wall, limp and shaking. The excuses she'd made for him didn't apply anymore. He obviously wasn't lying in a ditch hurt or dying. He was here. In Denver. And he looked absolutely marvelous.

The jerk.

So why hadn't he called her? Hell, he wasn't the fool, she was. She jammed a fist against the wall. History repeats itself. She was the story of her mother all over again. A one-night stand for an arrogant, sexy playboy. Her mother had been right and like a fool, she hadn't listened.

Ginger forced herself to take deep, even breaths. She was hyperventilating and close to a full-blown panic attack. Out of nowhere a hand clamped on her shoulder. A scream escaped her lips, ringing out loudly into the vacant building. Ginger's hand flew to her chest to still the wild beating of her heart.

Looking up, she discovered one of the clean-up crew staring at her with worry in his eyes. She knocked his hand off her shoulder as if it was a hairy spider. Hysterical laughter spilled out of her. She'd thought for a split second Vince had been the one to round the corner.

"Are you alright?"

"Yes . . . no . . . I will be. Just let me catch my breath. You scared me. Do you always sneak up on people like that?" she accused.

"I called out your name twice. You didn't hear me."

A slow burn traveled up Ginger's cheeks. She'd been so busy wallowing in self-pity over Vince she hadn't heard anything. "Sorry," she muttered.

"You don't look so good," the man informed her. "Why don't you take a break and let me finish this floor for you?"

"No, I'm fine. That's not necessary." Ginger looked up. Her gaze was drawn to a placard mounted to a massive oak door. The engraved sign read "Vince Danelli, President." What would she find if she went in there and cleaned his office? Would there be a picture of his latest conquest on his desk? Ginger was sure the woman would be beautiful with a smile on her lips and love shining in her eyes. Or maybe she'd find notches in his chair for every love-starved female he'd conquered. She cursed under her breath.

Robyn had delegated Ginger to be in charge. Yet she was so out of control of the situation she couldn't even think coherently. Five minutes. That's all she needed to get hold of her faculties. Five lousy minutes. "All right. You can do it."

"I need your keys."

Ginger stuck her hand in her pocket and felt the heavy weight of the key ring. The cold steel contrasted sharply with her sweaty palm. How did she know she could trust this guy? "What's your name?"

"Johnson. John Johnson."

"How long have you worked here?"

"Not long, but long enough. Relax. Robyn wouldn't have hired me if I didn't know what I was doing." He smiled at her. He looked sincere.

Of their own volition, Ginger's gaze moved to the placard again. She couldn't go into Vince's office. With a jingle, she brought the keys out of her pocket and put them in John's outstretched hand. "Okay.

But do that office first." She pointed to Vince's door with a shaky hand. "And do a bang-up job. I'm told the man is . . . hard to please."

"Why didn't you tell me?" Ginger asked, her voice deceptively mild considering that anger was pulsing through her veins like molten lava.

"Oh, my God, Ginger. Do you actually believe I would have sent you there if I had known the president of the company was *your* Vince?" Robyn paced the vinyl floor of Ginger's kitchen, her movements jerky with agitation.

"He's not *my* Vince. And I don't know what I believe anymore." Ginger placed her forehead against the cold window pane. The snow fell silently to the ground covering their corner of the world in a blanket of glistening white.

"I never knew your . . . sorry . . . Vince's last name anyway. This is too much of a weird coincidence."

Ginger's heart constricted in her chest. *Do you believe in fate?* Vince's words burned in her memory as a shiver ran down her spine. "There's no such thing as coincidence," she whispered.

Robyn stopped pacing and stood in front

of the window next to her. "What are you talking about?"

"Fate," Ginger laughed. "Kismet, destiny. Pick whatever name you want to call it. Everything happens for a reason."

"You're seriously flaking out on me."

Turning, Ginger looked her friend in the eye. "Think about it. My mother meets a handsome man, falls hard for him and then ends up pregnant and alone. I meet a handsome man, fall hard for him —"

"You're pregnant?" Robyn shouted.

Eyes closed, Ginger envisioned holding a baby of Vince's in her arms. With dark hair and brilliant green eyes, the child would be beautiful. "No. We took precaution." Was that regret she heard in her own voice?

Robyn hit her on the shoulder. "That's not fate. That's your mother brainwashing you since the day you were in diapers against the evils of man . . . any man." She threw her hands up in the air. "I'm surprised you ever got engaged to Steven." Robyn walked away from the window then turned around and stalked back.

Anger glittered in her eyes and her stance remained rigid, but her words were calmer, quieter. "I know you're hurting. I feel for you, I really do. But welcome to the real world, Ginger. You've just experienced what most women learn a lot earlier in life. If you had ever let yourself feel any kind of emotion, you would have learned that a long time ago."

Let herself feel emotion? Hadn't she accused her mother of the very same thing only weeks ago? She was more like Eva Thompson than she'd ever imagined. With a fist full of curtain in her grip, Ginger swallowed past the lump in her throat. Robyn's words stung, but she refused to accept what her friend said. Ginger had been engaged to Steven so she must have loved him. Love was an emotion. Hence, Robyn was wrong. "I just hope I never see Vince again," she muttered.

"I know, kid. I know."

Christmas came and went. In the past it had always been Ginger's favorite holiday. This year she found no joy in the season. All she could remember was Vince telling her he wanted to spend Christmas with her.

Yet she spent the majority of it alone.

Going to her mother's had been torture. Ginger desperately longed for the comfort only a mother can give to mend her aching heart. But afraid her mother would say "I told you so" if she confessed Vince had dumped her just like she'd predicted,

Ginger couldn't utter a single word. In the end, she'd pleaded the flu and went home early. Crawling under the down comforter on her bed like a wounded animal, Ginger had hugged her pillow to her chest and cried herself to sleep.

After another week of living in a haze, Ginger knew she had to accept the truth for what it was and get on with living.

Vince wasn't coming back.

She'd declined at first when Robyn had wanted to set her up with a date for New Year's Eve, but then she changed her mind. Ginger's resolution for the new year was, she decided, not to prove her mother was right, but to prove to herself another man did exist who could make her feel emotions the way Vince's touch had.

"Darling, could you get me another drink?"

Vince looked down at the gorgeous redhead on his arm and smiled. "Of course, Cynthia." Reaching out, he pulled a champagne glass off the tray of a passing uniformed waiter and pressed it into her neatly manicured hand.

Now here was a woman who knew how to please a man, Vince thought. Cynthia didn't argue with him. Cynthia didn't make him angry. Cynthia agreed with everything he said.

Cynthia was pretty damn boring.

But she was about as opposite from Ginger as a woman could get. And at this point, what he needed more than anything was to forget. He *had* to erase the memory of the most incredible woman he'd ever met in his life. After three weeks, he still couldn't figure out what had gone wrong. When he'd gone to call Ginger, the piece of paper she'd given him with her number on it had been blank.

Information had never heard of a Ginger Cooper, unlisted or otherwise. He'd called every modeling agency in town to no avail. It was as if she'd never existed, as if she was a figment of his imagination, a dream that had burst when he'd come back to reality.

"You promised me a dance, darling," Cynthia purred with a slight pout to her brightly painted lips, her body pressing close against his.

Vince thought going out on New Year's would help revive his spirits. But when he pulled the heavily perfumed woman into his arms on the crowded dance floor, all he could think of was Ginger. Determined to make himself ignore his longing for her, he pulled Cynthia closer. The gold lamé dress she wore clung to her body, exposing more than a little of her generous anatomy to his view.

What he needed was to feel another woman writhing beneath him to make him forget. Ginger wasn't the first woman to make him hard, and he vowed she wouldn't be the last. "What do you say we get out of here?" He whispered the suggestion against her ear.

The woman looked up at him through long lashes he was sure were fake. "But it's not even midnight yet."

He ran a hand down her back and squeezed her fleshy rump. "We don't need hundreds of other people to help us celebrate, do we?"

"Oh," she cooed, understanding finally dawning in her pale green eyes. Cynthia grabbed his arm, pulled him off the dance floor and made her way through the throngs of people to the coat checkroom.

Vince smiled to himself. An eager, willing woman was exactly what he needed. Wrapping her fur coat around her, Vince let his hands brush against the sides of her breasts. He felt nothing. No rush of excitement. No catching of his breath. No lust. Nothing.

Dispassionately, he watched her eyes fill

with desire and anticipation. Maybe it was the atmosphere. He was sure he'd feel *something* when he got her to his apartment. He hoped she was as eager in bed as she appeared.

Whisking her around, he ushered her out of the doors of the restaurant and onto the crowded Denver streets. Ready to hail a cab, the echo of familiar laughter caught his attention. For one heart-stopping moment, he thought he'd heard the sound of Ginger's voice. Scanning the crowds of partyers lining the sidewalks, he found her smiling face across a sea of people.

"Ginger," he whispered, his breath a puff of white smoke in the chilly air. He dropped Cynthia's hand and started to cross the street, but the blond entered a limo on the arm of another man.

"Ginger," he called out louder. But it was too late. The black limo whisked her away and out of his life again. His racing heart slowed to a steady, painful thud against his chest. He prayed it would stop beating altogether. He didn't need it.

"Viiince," Cynthia whined. "I'm cold. Can we go?" She rubbed her breasts against his arm in a gesture he found repugnant.

Putting his fingers to his lips, he whistled

for a cab. When it stopped in front of him, he opened the door and ushered his date in. Dropping a fifty on the front seat he said, "Take her wherever she wants to go."

"What's going on, Vince?" Her long, red nails dug into his sleeve like the claws of a cat.

Vince shook her hand off with distaste.

"I thought we were going to . . . celebrate?" Cynthia let her fur coat fall open, exposing Vince to a full view of her scantily covered breasts.

Vince closed his eyes to the memory of another woman wearing a red ski parka with a beige teddy underneath. "I've changed my mind," he growled. Slamming the door, he stood rooted to the spot as the yellow cab sped away. Cynthia's pouting face stared at him through the back window like that of a petulant child.

A clock on the tower above Vince rang out the hour of midnight. Around him everyone yelled out "Happy New Year" as confetti drifted through the night sky like falling snow.

The crowd pushed and jostled around him, but Vince felt as if he was the only person left on the face of the earth. Who the hell was he trying to kid? he asked himself, jamming his fists into his pockets, his shoulders hunched against the cold. No one could ever take Ginger's place; not last year, not this new year, not ever.

"This has got to be the worst year of my life!" Robyn exclaimed, breezing into Ginger's living room.

"All three days of it?" Ginger asked trying to hide a smile.

"This isn't funny." Robyn stopped pacing long enough to dump her winter coat on a chair. She waved a crisp piece of folded paper in the air and opened her mouth, but nothing came out. In a movement that bespoke utter defeat and helplessness, Robyn sank onto the sofa and held her head in her hands.

A tingle of apprehension started at the base of Ginger's spine. "What's the matter with you?" Ginger snatched the document out of Robyn's fist. Her gaze scanned the top of the page. The word "subpoena" jumped out in bold, black letters.

"What's going on?"

Robyn lifted her head up and gazed at Ginger with tears in her eyes. "I'm being sued," she laughed nervously.

"Why?" Ginger sank on the cushion next to her friend. "I don't understand."

"You're never going to believe this,"

Robyn shook her head, a dark, snow-soaked curl clinging to her cheek.

"Try me."

She took a deep breath. "It seems, allegedly of course," she added sarcastically. "I stole documents of some sort out of one of the tenant's offices."

"Well, we both know you never did anything like that."

Robyn laughed a harsh laugh. "You're damn right we know it, because I was in Colorado Springs that night with Rick. It's the night you were there, Ginger. And it was none other than Vince Danelli's office."

Chapter 6

Even with the air conditioning blasting full force, Ginger's silk blouse stuck to her sweaty back from the August midday heat beating in through the car window. I-25 had become a parking lot instead of a highway.

She was late. And there was *nothing* Ginger hated more than being late.

Taking her exit, she found a parking spot in a crowded lot, grabbed her purse off the seat next to her and rushed across the street to the courthouse. Ginger still couldn't believe her ex-fiancé, Steven, had agreed to represent Robyn in this case. He certainly didn't have to. Not after the way Ginger had dumped him almost a year ago. As easy as she'd tried to make it on him, he'd been hurt.

When she entered Steven's office, his secretary placed a hand over the mouthpiece of the phone she was talking into and whispered, "They're waiting for you, Ms. Thompson." She pointed to a closed door.

Ginger entered the office and immediately felt the glare from two sets of eyes upon her.

"You're late," Robyn and Steven accused at the same time.

"Traffic." Ginger supplied, taking a leather seat next to her friend. There had never been any love lost between these two people. Leaving them in a closed room was like leaving Tweety alone with Sylvester.

"The trial starts in a half hour, Ginger. That doesn't leave us much time to review," Steven said.

A half hour. It was hard to believe in such a short amount of time she'd be seeing Vince again. "How did it get pushed through in eight months anyway? I thought it took years before cases like this actually even made it to the courtroom." Ginger wanted to get it over with, she really did. But the thought of seeing Vince had her stomach rolling and her head pounding.

"It's called rock 'em and sock 'em," Robyn answered.

A weary sigh escaped Steven. He pushed his hand through his impeccably cut hair and Ginger thought it looked like he would much rather use that hand to strangle Robyn.

"It's — called — a — Rocket — Docket,"

Steven said between clenched teeth. He tilted his head back and stared at the ceiling.

"Well, excuuuuse me. I guess I flunked out of Lawyer Lingo 101," Robyn retorted.

The traffic, the heat, and her apprehension about the events to come made Ginger lose what small amount of self-control she had left. "Hey," she yelled. Jumping up from her chair, she hit the top of the desk with the palms of her hands.

Steven and Robyn both flinched, then looked at her with surprise planted across their faces. It was exactly the reaction she was hoping for.

"Now that I have your attention, let's save the fighting for the courtroom, shall we?" Ginger felt like a schoolteacher with two undisciplined children on her hands. "I thought we were all on the same side? Can we *please* act like it?" She saw the angry looks Robyn and Steven exchanged, but chose to ignore it.

"I'm the one who's going to end up in jail. What are you so upset about?" Robyn asked.

Steven leaned back in his chair, a small smile playing about his lips as if he thoroughly enjoyed the thought of the woman in front of him spending time behind bars. "You won't end up incarcerated," he admitted. "If you're found guilty, there will probably be a first injunction and you'll have to swear never to do it again."

"I didn't do it in the first place." Sarcasm edged Robyn's every word. "And believe me, no one will ever give me a chance to do it again. Owning a company with a lawsuit on its hands doesn't exactly instill trust in potential customers."

They were best friends, yet Ginger had never realized Robyn was having such a difficult time making ends meet. Ginger felt as guilty as if she *had* been the one to steal the designs out of Vince's office. She sat back down on the chair and looked her in the eye. "You never told me things were getting so hard."

Robyn laughed and shrugged her shoulders. "It's not that bad. I still have a few small contracts to fulfill. I'm getting used to macaroni and cheese anyway. You'd be surprised what a little imagination can do to the stuff." She rolled her eyes and averted her gaze out the window.

Guilt burned Ginger from the roots of her hair to the tips of her toes. The theft had supposedly occurred while she was in charge. She knew Robyn trusted her. But sometimes all the faith in the world wasn't enough. They had to prove Robyn innocent.

Or die trying. "Let's get down to business and win this case."

"Great. Nothing would make me happier. And when we do, there will be steak and lobster in my macaroni and cheese for everybody."

Dread lodged an immovable lump in Ginger's throat, and made her want to turn around and flee. But she couldn't. Robyn's future depended on her testimony. With more fortitude than she felt, Ginger squared her shoulders and opened the massive door in front of her.

Full of people, the courtroom buzzed with noise.

"Wow, would you look at this place," Robyn said. "What a circus." She moved in front of Ginger and headed up the aisle toward her seat at the defendant's table.

Ginger wanted to follow, but her legs wouldn't cooperate. A sixth sense warned her of his presence, an invisible radar Ginger would much rather have not possessed.

Vince was here.

Above the heads of the people milling about the room, she saw him. Her breath caught in her throat, and her heart accelerated. With his back to her, Vince's dark hair curled over his stark white shirt; his shoulders stretched impossibly wide beneath his dark business suit.

When she reached the gate separating the crowd of observers from the lawyers, judge, and jury she stopped. It had been nine months since she'd last seen him. Nine months of pretending she'd forgotten. Nine months of trying to erase his memory from her mind. Nine very long months of wasted time.

He was exactly like the Vince she imagined every night before she drifted off to sleep. Handsome, muscular, sexy, undeniably male.

Slowly turning his head, his gaze slammed into hers. "Ginger," she saw his mouth whisper. He took a hesitant step toward her.

Ginger placed a hand on the swinging gate ready to push it open. She wanted to fling herself into his arms. To hell with the fact he'd never called her. He was here now, and the look burning in his eyes said he was happy to see her. For Ginger, it was more than enough.

A cold hand gripped her forearm and pulled her away from Vince. "Come on. We need to take our seats." Robyn dragged Ginger against her will to the first row in the gallery behind Steven.

When she looked back at Vince, his face had paled beneath his tan. Frigid disbelief replaced the welcoming look in his eyes. There could be no denying she was sitting behind the attorney for the defense. And he was the plaintiff. She watched as a wall of indifference rose around him. All except for the muscle ticking in his jaw he appeared composed, relaxed, detached; a man unaffected by his surroundings.

If only Ginger could emulate him. But she couldn't. Her body had turned into a quivering mass of raw nerves. Why had Robyn chosen that exact moment to pull her aside? Just two more seconds and Ginger would have had Vince's arms wrapped around her.

She sighed in disgust. Why get a taste for something she couldn't have? Whether it happened now or in five minutes or when she took the stand, he would find out. She was on the other side, an enemy in his eyes even if she was innocent. Ginger was somebody to be avoided at all costs.

"Who," Robyn asked, squeezing her arm, "is that?" She nodded in Vince's direction.

Ginger didn't look up. "It's Vince."

"Not him. The hunk next to him."

"I don't know." She refused to turn her head in Vince's direction.

Having overheard their conversation, Steven turned around. "*That* is none other than David Michaels. DePaul University Law School. Graduated top of the class. Lost only one case his entire career. He's good, ladies. Real good."

"He *looks* good. Incredibly . . . good." Robyn's voice held the dreamy quality of a woman ready to fall head over heels in love.

Ginger clucked in disgust. "Do you ever think about anything else?"

"Hey, I'm not dead."

"Vince Danelli must have some pretty strong connections," Steven supplied. "David Michaels doesn't take just *any* client. He has a reputation for being ruthless, demanding, and domineering. The guy likes to win."

Ginger thought he sounded exactly like Vince.

"Does that apply only in the courtroom or out of it also?" Robyn questioned.

Ginger had had enough. How could they carry on as if nothing was happening? Her world was falling down around her and these two were acting as if they were taking a Sunday stroll through the park. "I'm going to be sick," she complained, her stomach churning.

"I know what you mean," Robyn said. "I feel kind of queasy myself."

With a hand to her mouth, Ginger leapt out of her chair and ran to the ladies' room.

It was the seventh grade all over again. Vince had gotten into a fight and had the wind knocked out of him. But he couldn't catch his breath. Fighting for air, his thoughts tumbled over one another. Why was Ginger here? What did she have to do with the theft of his designs? She was obviously involved if she was sitting behind the defense.

The sound of a chair scraping behind him caught his attention. Try as he might, Vince couldn't stop himself from turning to watch as Ginger ran from the room, a hand clenched over her mouth and her face as pale as a sheet. It served her right if she was sick. He closed his eyes, sinking down onto his hard wooden chair.

He hurt. His entire body ached. Never had he suffered such an overwhelming sense of loss, betrayal, or loneliness in his entire life. Not even when he'd tried to track Ginger down and couldn't find her. This was much worse. To know she was here, but not to be able to touch her or hold her. His hopes of continuing where they'd left off shattered into a thousand pieces.

Damn women.

Damn women to hell and back again. He should have known better than to let himself fall for any female after his breakup with Liz. But Ginger had seemed different. Vulnerable, somehow.

He wanted to throw his head back and laugh out loud. Vulnerable? The woman had played him for a fool from the very beginning. God but she was good. He remembered back to the weekend he met her. He had advanced and she had retreated. What an act. She must have known her refusal of his attentions would only make him want her more. It had worked. A man couldn't have desired a woman more than Vince had craved Ginger.

But nothing explained why she did it. Why would she want a top-secret architectural design? Did she do it for the money? Who did she work for?

He would have expected something like this from his old nemesis, Renard Duchaine. The very thought of the name made his fists clench. The man had tried for years to outsmart Vince. They consistently placed bids on the same contracts. Vince usually won, leaving Duchaine vowing to get even. Every attempt he'd tried had failed. Yes, this plan reeked of Duchaine. No matter what it took, Vince would prove he was involved.

The hairs on the back of his neck stood on end. Ginger was back. He knew without even looking, which he refused to do. He wouldn't give her the satisfaction of knowing she could still get to him. Damn women anyway.

"All rise for the honorable Judge Winston," the bailiff called out. A hush traveled over the crowd, quieting voices to a whispered level.

"This is it. Are you ready?" Vince's lawyer, David Michaels asked of him.

"Ready as I'll ever be," he replied. Pushing his chair back, he stood.

The judge entered the room with a swish of her long, black robe. A woman! The judge was a woman. His fate once again depended on the whim of a female. Vince closed his eyes and rubbed his forehead. The odds were definitely against him.

Ginger turned off the shower, pulled on a lavender housecoat and wrapped a matching towel around her damp hair.

"I'm coming, I m coming," she yelled out, leaving a trail of water from the bathroom to the front door. The buzzer rang incessantly.

Robyn had left Ginger's house twenty minutes earlier to go to the store in search of much-needed ice cream to indulge in. Why didn't she just use her key to let herself in? Unlocking the door, she pulled it open with a twist of the knob.

"Lay off the bell, Robyn. I hear you already."

Ginger gasped as the door was forced open and banged against the wall with a thud. Vince stood on the threshold larger than life, utterly masculine and wearing a look colder than an iceberg in the Antarctic.

"Why?" he asked through clenched teeth.

She backed away from the fury burning in that one word until the solid wall stopped her. There was nowhere left to go. Nowhere to hide. "I had nothing to do with the theft, Vince. You have to believe me."

"Save it for the judge," he growled. Advancing a step, he slammed the door closed behind him.

Ginger's heart beat rapidly in her chest. She watched him survey the room. Why was he here? How had he found her?

"Nice home you have."

She could tell by the sarcastic tone of his voice he wasn't paying her a compliment.

"I wonder how you can afford it on a secretary's salary."

Ginger stood up taller. How could he know her occupation or salary? Was he checking up on her as if she were a common criminal? "What did you do, hire a private investigator?"

Slowly his head turned and his brilliant green eyes met hers. She flinched at the naked loathing and disbelief reflected there.

"It pays to know as much about your adversaries as you can," he said, his voice almost a whisper.

The intended jab hit its mark and Ginger felt it. But she'd be damned if she'd let him know it. Lifting her chin a notch, she fought back the tears burning at her eyes. Anger slowly rose to the surface. Saving for her dream home had taken years of pinching pennies and going without. She was innocent, damn it. "I don't have to explain anything to you. I've worked hard for what I've got."

Vince stood so close Ginger could feel the heat from his body. "Yeah. Lying on your back takes a lot of energy, doesn't it?"

The heat of humiliation flooded her cheeks. "You bastard!" Out of instinct Ginger swung her hand toward his face. He caught it firmly in his grip a second before impact. His nostrils flared in anger, but he didn't say a word. Instead he flung her hand away from him as if the contact burned his skin.

With her heart beating in an erratic tempo, she watched Vince move to the middle of the living room, his hands tight-fisted at his sides. It was as if he couldn't trust himself to come any closer to her. The wild look in his eyes terrified her. Ginger clutched her robe tightly against her chest, her hand shaking with the fear building inside her.

"Who do you work for?" he demanded.

"The Tyler Agency."

"Jesus," Vince ran a hand through his dark hair. "No. I mean who paid you to steal those designs out of my office?"

When would he believe she didn't do it? "I don't work for anyone. No one paid me. I've never done anything against the law in my life. I don't even like to lie." Ginger closed her eyes, realizing her mistake too late. The time she'd been with him in Steamboat had been nothing but one distorted truth on top of another.

He knew it and she knew it.

Regardless of her true feelings for the man standing in front of her, he would never see her as anything but what she appeared to be — a deceitful woman. And that, she reminded herself, was the one thing he had said he found unforgivable in any human being.

When she opened her eyes again he was standing directly in front of her. She smelled his masculine scent, breathed in deeply. He was close enough to touch if she only dared. "The night I met you was the first time I ever lied in my life. How can I make you understand it had absolutely nothing to do with you?" She looked deeply into his eyes, begging him to accept what she was trying to tell him.

He stared back, the coldness of his expression chilling her to the bone.

"Robyn and I were just trying to have some fun," she continued. "She accused me of being a stick in the mud and I wanted to prove her wrong. Mostly because I knew how right she was. My life has always been neat and orderly and precise and . . . and very boring." When she dared to look at him, he stood with his hands on his hips, his mouth in a tight line.

Well, Ginger, it's certainly not boring now. "It was Robyn's idea to change our careers and our identities. I'm not blaming her. I guess I went right along with the idea. It seemed like . . . I don't know . . . fun." She tightened the sash around her waist and self-consciously touched the towel turban on her head. "If I had known that one little white lie would have caused so much trouble I wouldn't have ever told it." Ginger looked up at him imploringly. Even angry he was exceedingly handsome. Her heart constricted in her chest, robbing her of much-needed air.

Very handsome.

And very much lost to her.

She licked her dry lips. "I tried to tell you the truth about who I really was," she whispered.

"When?" He laughed harshly. "When I told you I had never met a woman like you before? When I held you in my arms, when you forced yourself to return my kisses, or was it when I took you to my bed?"

"I . . ." Ginger blinked back a flood of tears. "I didn't have to force myself, Vince. I liked your kisses."

"Which kisses did you like, Ginger?" Vince wrapped an arm about her waist and roughly hauled her tight against his warm chest. He kissed her softly on her mouth. The almost tender touch belied the steely feel of his arm about her. "Did you like that kiss?"

Before she could answer, his head came down again and he gently bit her lip and then kissed her soundly as his free hand loosened the belt and slipped inside her robe. He rubbed the sensitive skin of her stomach, still damp from the shower. Long-restrained longing snaked through her.

"Or maybe you liked that one better." Roughly, his lips possessed hers. The towel slipped from her head and landed in a puddle at her bare feet.

Ginger knew she should put up some sort of resistance. But it was as if the past nine months faded away. They were back in the hotel in Steamboat Springs, and she was eager to make love with the man of her dreams.

She opened her mouth on a sigh and his tongue slipped inside. She couldn't deny the passion, didn't even want to. Her body burned from head to toe and back up again. Vince cupped her breast in his hand and Ginger wrapped her arms around his neck to pull him closer as her tongue met his. She gave him kiss for kiss, and answered his burning desire with her own. She had never known a need so raw.

As quickly as it started, Vince shoved her away. Ginger's robe hung open and he stared at her heaving breasts while he wiped his mouth with the back of his hand.

"Or maybe you like it rough." With a click

of disgust he turned on his heel, opened the door and slammed it shut behind him.

The house was eerily silent as Ginger pulled the edges of her robe together with shaking hands. Slowly she slid against the wall to the floor and wrapped her arms around her bent knees. She hugged herself into a tight ball. "I like all your kisses, Vince," she whispered as the dam broke and the harsh sobs began. "I like them all."

Chapter 7

A strong wind whipped through the trees as Vince stood on the front stoop of Ginger's house. The bleak sound matched the howling loneliness inside him. Kissing her had been a mistake. He'd wanted to prove to himself contempt was the only emotion driving him. But he knew that wasn't true.

Vince wanted Ginger just as much now as he had before. How the hell could he want a woman he didn't trust? Out of exasperation and anger he punched the brick wall, only serving to add throbbing knuckles to his list of miseries.

Through the closed door, he could hear her muted sobs. He wanted to go to her, take her in his arms; beg her forgiveness. Hesitantly he set foot on the welcome mat. He drew himself up short, stifling a laugh. He would be about as welcome as a box of rattlesnakes. And Vince sure as hell hadn't done anything to be forgiven for, anyway. Clenching a fist, he steeled his heart against the sound of her crying, kept his jaw rigid.

She was an actress. A flawless, lying, Oscar-winning actress. If he could get his hands on one of the gold statues, he'd mail it to her.

Reluctant to leave, yet not wanting to stay, Vince moved off the stoop and walked a few steps into the darkness, away from the bright light on the porch. In time he would forget Ginger, he told himself. Forget the way her body melded to his when they'd made love. Forget the taste of her honeyed lips. Forget the shape of her seductive smile and the desire burning in her beautiful blue eyes.

You've had nine months to forget her, buddy. What makes you think you can do it this time? Ah, but he knew the truth about her now. The Ginger crying on the other side of the door wasn't the Ginger he thought he knew. She was an impostor. A mere shell of the woman he'd fallen in love with.

Forgetting *her* would be easy. After all, hadn't she been just a one-night stand, a mindless diversion on a weekend trip? A muscle ticked in his jaw and he cursed his own weakness. A car pulled into the driveway. Vince remained rooted to the spot, hidden in the dark shadows of he trees. His heart thumped in his chest. Did Ginger have another lover arriving already? Someone to take her into his arms, patch up her wounded ego? Not that he should care, he reminded himself, but he did.

The car door slammed and footsteps walked up the path. Almost upon him, Vince chose that moment to walk out of the shadows and into the light from the porch. The dark-haired woman before him gasped and dropped her sack of groceries on the ground, spilling the contents in several directions. A can rolled down the sidewalk, then clanked down the steps. The hollow noise echoed into the darkness.

"What the hell are you doing here?" she asked, a hand to her chest.

Ignoring his relief that it was Ginger's friend, Robyn, and not a man, Vince took in the accusing glare in her eyes. "Damned if I know." He bent down and picked up an item from the ground. He raised an eyebrow and thrust a container of chocolate ice cream at the woman. "A little premature for a celebration, don't you think?"

She grabbed the article from his hands and clutched it to her chest. "You're not supposed to be here." She looked toward the door where muffled sounds of Ginger's crying could still be heard. Her pupils widened, her lips parted as a tiny gasp escaped her. She advanced toward Vince like a mother bear defending her young. "What did you do to her? Did you hurt her?" Her eyes narrowed dangerously.

Vince stood his ground despite the sharp finger poking in his chest. "All her wounds are self-inflicted." He walked around the groceries scattered at his feet, and strolled away without a backward glance.

"Could you please tell the court how you know these two . . . ladies?"

The slight hesitation before the word "ladies" was almost imperceptible. But Vince caught it, knew the judge, the jury and everyone else in the courtroom caught it, too. "I met them on a ski trip to Steamboat Springs."

"And do you ski there often?"

"Never. I won the tickets in a contest."

"Contest?" David Michaels, attorney for the plaintiff, questioned. "You mean you were, say, tenth caller on a radio show?"

"No. The tickets came in the mail. I don't remember ever entering a drawing, though. I thought it was a hoax."

"Why did you go, then?"

"I knew I would be moving to Denver shortly. I wanted to explore the rest of the state. Get a feel for it."

"I see. And how did you meet these two?" The lawyer gestured to Ginger and Robyn.

Vince refused to look at them. His earlier peek at Ginger had been enough. Her eyes were red and puffy, her face pale. Even the light pink suit she wore failed to put color on her cheeks. "The first night I arrived," he began, "I checked in and went down to the bar for a beer. As soon as I walked in I felt someone staring a me."

"Staring at you? How?"

"You know, checking me out. It was Ginger. She was very attractive. I asked her to dance." Vince tried to shut out the memory of her pliant body in his arms. *What's your name?* he'd asked. *Don't tell me yours. Let me guess.* It was then the realization hit him. "God, I just remembered. She knew my name. I didn't have to tell her. She said she wanted to guess and she did. She had to have known who I was." The conniving little bitch. God, why hadn't he seen all this before? How could he be so stupid to let a woman dupe him yet again?

Vince's gaze snapped to Ginger's. She stared back, her eyes wide, like a thief caught in her own trap. "To make a long story short, when I pursued her she pretended not to be interested. When I gave up the fight, she was all over me." Vince never

140

took his gaze off Ginger even though she'd lowered her eyes and appeared to be studying the tabletop.

"Could you please explain to the court what 'all over you' implies?"

"Just like it sounds. We had sex." A muscle ticked in his jaw. It had been much more than that. It had been an awakening to the realization that this was how it was meant to be between a man and a woman. An exploding of the senses, a feeling he'd never had before and knew he'd never feel again.

Ginger looked up, her tear-filled gaze locking with his. If he didn't know any better, he could almost believe the tears were real. He tore his gaze away. He couldn't look at her another second. Not now. Not knowing that the *act* had been performed out of duty. That it really was nothing but the cheap sex he'd implied it was.

"And then what happened?" his lawyer questioned.

"I asked for her phone number. She wrote it on a piece of paper, but when I got home, the number was gone."

"Are you sure she actually wrote it down?"

"Very sure. I looked at the numbers before I slipped it into my wallet. It was as if she used disappearing ink or something. I tried Information next, but they didn't have a listing under her name. I tried tracking her down at modeling agencies, but Ginger Cooper didn't exist." Vince vividly remembered the pain when he realized he couldn't find her. Even knowing her for the fraud she was, it still hurt. All his insides seemed to be twisted into one big knot.

"I thought maybe she was a figment of my imagination, that she hadn't been real. But then I saw her on New Year's Eve. She was with another man, smiling and laughing, enjoying the holidays. A very happy woman. She'd gotten what she wanted from me and moved on to other prey."

"And what do you think she wanted from you?"

"Objection," the lawyer for the defense shouted out. "What he *thinks* she wanted is merely speculation."

"Your honor," Michaels pleaded, "The woman wasn't out to find love. I think Mr. Danelli's answer might shed some light on the situation."

"Overruled," the judge said.

"Again," David asked, "What did she want from you?"

"I think that's pretty obvious. She wanted

information about my business. She wanted to find out how easy it would be to get into my safe and steal my designs. She wanted to ruin my life."

"Objection!"

"Sustained. Mr. Danelli, please keep your answers aimed at the facts and not just assumptions." The judge fixed him with a stare of authority.

"Yes, your honor." At this moment, Vince wasn't sure if he could distinguish between fact and fiction. His head told him to move on with his life. Date a thousand other women if that's what it took to erase Ginger's memory. But his wounded heart wasn't about to listen to reason. How easy it would be to forget her, except that whenever he closed his eyes, he could see her, feel her, taste her. And he wanted her more than ever.

"No more questions, your honor."

"You may step down, Mr. Danelli."

"Do you swear to tell the truth, the whole truth and nothing but the truth, so help you God?"

The hand she placed on the Bible shook ever so slightly. "I do," Ginger answered.

"Please take a seat," the judge told her.

"Ms. Thompson, could you please tell us your full name?"

Ginger looked into the lawyer's eyes. Though compassion was lacking, he didn't appear as threatening as she thought he would. "My name's Ginger Ann Thompson."

"Have you ever gone by any other name?"

"No."

"Really?" David Michaels turned toward the jury, then back to her. A smile played about his lips that sent a shiver down Ginger's spine. "You've never gone by the name Ginger Cooper?"

"I . . . I . . ."

"Have you or haven't you?"

"It was a silly game." Ginger twisted her hands in her lap.

"A game?"

"Yes."

"Wasn't it more like a job? A job to trick my client, Vince Danelli, into falling for you in the hopes he would supply you with information while in the throes of passion?"

Horrified, Ginger yelled out, "No!"

"Then what was it, Ms. Thompson?"

"I don't know. I don't even remember now why we did it. But I know we planned to change our names before Vince came into that bar. I swear, I never heard of Vince Danelli before that night."

The lawyer placed a hand on either side of

the stand and leaned in so close Ginger could see her own reflection in his pupils.

"Then how," he asked, "did you know his name?"

She swallowed. "Robyn was standing by the front desk when he checked in. She overheard his name."

"How convenient that must have been for you. Does she always eavesdrop when people are checking in?"

"No. It was just coincidence, I'm sure."

He paced across the floor, then came back and stood in front of her. "Why were you in Steamboat?"

"To ski."

"Do you ski there often?"

"No. I can't ski worth a damn." The spectators chuckled and a slow flush burned across her cheeks.

"If you dislike skiing so much, why did you go?"

She knew no one would believe this part, but it was true. "Robyn won tickets."

"Just like Mr. Danelli did?"

She could see the shock in his eyes. "Yes."

"That was convenient, wasn't it?"

"No, it wasn't. Like I said, I hate skiing, but Robyn begged me to go. She's my best friend. I couldn't say no."

"So why did you sleep with him?"

Ginger swallowed. This man went right for the jugular. Her gaze skittered to Vince. Under oath, she knew she had to tell the truth, but it stuck in her throat.

"Ms. Thompson, you have to answer the question," the judge prodded gently from above her.

Ginger closed her eyes and took a deep, calming breath. "I was very attracted to him." Opening them again, she watched Vince's eyes narrow with what looked like disbelief. He thought she was lying. She lowered her head and stared at her hands. "I thought I was falling in love with him."

"You expect this courtroom to believe you'd fallen in love with a man you'd known less than two days?"

"Yes," she whispered.

"What was that, Ms. Thompson?"

Ginger stared at the lawyer, anger getting the better of her. "Yes," she said clearly. "I fell in love with him that fast. He is charming, kind, decent, and patient. He's handsome and sexy and so damn appealing I couldn't resist him, and believe me, I know because I tried." Realizing she'd said out loud what she'd only meant to think, she mumbled, "Any woman would have fallen for him."

"And you were so much in love that you

dumped him at the first opportunity. Isn't that correct?"

"I didn't dump him," she sighed in exasperation.

"Come now, Ms. Thompson. You wrote down your number with disappearing ink so he couldn't find you. If that isn't a woman who wants a man out of her life, what is?"

Ginger knew the lawyer was only doing his job, but she could have easily jumped out of her chair and ripped him apart limb by limb. She pierced him with what she hoped was one of her fiercest stares. "I didn't realize I was using a pen with disappearing ink."

"Please, humor us. Just how did it get into your possession?"

Sighing, Ginger continued her story. "I was looking for a pen and couldn't find one. Robyn carries everything under the sun in her purse, so I took one out of her bag."

"And you had never seen this pen before?"

She fidgeted in her seat. "Actually, yes I had."

"But you used it anyway, even knowing that it contained disappearing ink?"

"I was distracted. I couldn't think straight. I forgot."

"How were you distracted?"

Heat suffused her face. She glanced at Vince and then quickly looked away. She didn't want to see the hatred glazing in his eyes. "Vince was standing behind me nibbling on my . . . ," she lowered her voice to a mumbled whisper, "breast."

"Excuse me, Ms. Thompson. Speak up. I don't believe we all heard you."

Ginger cleared her throat. Never had she hated anyone with a white-hot passion like she did this man. She sat up straighter. "He was nibbling on my breast Mr. Michaels."

"You expect the jury to believe this in itself caused you to lose all sense of reason?"

An involuntary smile lifted the corners of her mouth at the memory. "You've obviously never had Vince Danelli nibbling on your breast."

The lawyer reddened. Laughter erupted in the room.

"You may step down, Ms. Thompson."

"I'm glad you asked me out to dinner, Steven. I don't think I could have gone home to an empty house. I really blew it today, didn't I?" Ginger asked, feeling utterly miserable.

"You told the truth, that's what counts. We'll have another chance tomorrow when

148

we put Robyn on the stand." He patted her hand resting atop the linen-covered table. "I told you David Michaels was tough, didn't I?"

Ginger rolled her eyes. "Yes, you did. I guess I just wasn't prepared to bare my soul to the world."

"You really love that guy Vince, don't you?"

A lump lodged in her throat making her voice husky. "Yeah, I do. Look," she whispered, fiddling with her silverware, blinking back tears. "Can we change the subject? You're going to smear my mascara," she said with an attempt at humor.

"Of course. Actually, I have an ulterior motive for asking you to dinner. There's something I want to run by you."

She caught the searching look in his eyes. Oh, God. Please don't let him want to start the relationship again. "Steven, I really don't —"

He held up a hand, interrupting her. "Just hear me out before you say anything."

"Okay." She hoped she sounded calm on the outside. Cold with dread, she knew she didn't want to hurt him twice. Steven was a good man. A dependable man. But her love belonged to another. Despite the fact Vince detested her, he was in full possession of her heart. It wasn't hers anymore to give away. It never would be.

"Damn," Steven flashed an embarrassed smile. "This was so easy when I rehearsed it." He cleared his throat and ran a shaky hand through his brown hair.

"I —" The waiter came to refill their wine glasses and a look of relief flashed across Steven's face at the interruption.

"What would you think of me getting married?" he rushed in when they were alone again.

Oh, God, it was worse than she had feared. How could she let him down gently? He was a dear friend, but that was all. "Steven, we've tried this already. It didn't work the first time. It's not going to work now."

When Steven started laughing, her gaze snapped to his. "What's so funny?" she asked, puzzled by his reaction.

"I didn't mean *us* getting married. I meant *me* to someone else. I've met the most incredible woman, Gin. Actually incredible doesn't even begin to describe her." He grabbed her hands. "We're perfect for each other. I've asked her to marry me. Would you believe she said yes?"

Tears sprang to Ginger's eyes. "Of course I believe it. She must be one smart woman."

Why couldn't I have fallen for you, Steven? "I'm thrilled for you." And she was, but it was bittersweet. Ginger wondered if the empty feeling inside her would ever be filled with happiness.

But this was Steven's moment, not hers. She pushed the self-pity aside and reached across the table. With both hands cupping his face, she leaned over and planted a friendly kiss on his lips. "When's the big day?"

A light twinkled in his eyes. "As soon as this case is over, we're eloping. We don't want a big wedding. We just want to be husband and wife."

"She's one very lucky woman."

The hostess appeared at their table. "I'm sorry to interrupt. Are you Steven James?" she asked.

"Yes, I am." A look of worry jumped into his eyes.

"There's a phone call for you up front."

"Thank you." Taking his napkin off his lap, Steven set it on the table. "Excuse me, Ginger. I told my secretary I'd be here. She wouldn't call unless it was important. I'll be right back."

Ginger smiled at him and toyed with her wine glass while she waited for him to return. Out of the corner of her eye, she noticed a couple walking across the room. Something about the man's stride caught her attention. When she looked up, Vince, arm in arm with a buxom brunette, filled her vision.

He whispered to the woman. Ginger caught the words "meet you up front" above the music wafting through the speakers. The coppery taste of blood filled her mouth. She realized she was biting the inside of her cheek as an intense wave of jealousy washed over her. The couple separated, their fingertips touching in an intimate gesture until their distance pulled them completely apart.

An uncontrollable shiver ran down Ginger's spine. It wasn't just jealousy, but envy eating at her. It could have been her arm in arm with Vince, sharing touches and caresses and intimate glances. But all because of stupid mistakes, and stupider lies, it wasn't and never would be.

After the woman practically bursting from the confines of her black, skin-tight dress flitted past her, Vince strolled to Ginger's side. A sardonic smile twisted his lips. He placed his hands on the edge of the table and leaned down, his face within inches of hers.

As always, he looked impeccable in a dark

business suit. Ginger longed to touch him, to run her fingers through his hair, and trace the frown lines on either side of his sensuous mouth. She clenched her fists in her lap to restrain herself.

"What happened to your declaration of undying love for me?" he questioned, one eyebrow raised.

Ginger's heart skidded to a stop in her chest and then beat at a frantic pace. Puzzled, she searched his eyes, not finding any answers. "What do you mean?"

"On the stand today you said under oath that you loved me." A cold, bitter laugh escaped him. "Didn't take you long to look elsewhere."

Dread filled her chest. "What do you mean?"

"That little scene I just witnessed between you and your lawyer was quite touching. Do you think it's smart to be so public with your affections during the trial?"

She didn't need to hear the sarcastic tone in his voice to know he didn't mean a word he said. "I was congratulating Steven on some good news." Vince's stare was black. Against her will, she cupped a hand along his jawline, reveling in the feel of his whisker-rough skin and the pulse beating beneath her fingertips. It was a heavenly torture to touch him. "But you'll never under-stand that, will you? You only believe what you want to believe. If you tripped over the truth, you wouldn't know it."

A look flashed in Vince's eyes, one that conveyed an unmistakable warmth and ten-derness, reminding Ginger of the magical moments they'd shared in Steamboat. He quickly veiled it behind brittle coldness and she wondered if she'd just imagined the ex-pression.

"Oh, come now, Ms. *Thompson.* We both know the truth here. I'm sure you thought a few touches, a few well-placed kisses would lower your lawyer's fee tremendously. And if that doesn't work, you can always take him to your bed. It seems to be your specialty."

Hot rage filled every fiber of her body. This man would never understand anything about her, never believe the truth no matter what she said or did. Her hands shook as she grabbed her wine glass. With utter con-tempt, she flung the contents in his face. "You bastard!"

Red wine dripped down his astonished face. Pushing past him and rushing out of the restaurant, she realized calling Vince names was becoming an all too familiar habit.

Chapter 8

"Ginger, wait up." Steven rushed toward her, the sound of his wingtips echoing against the tiled floor of the courthouse hallway. "Where did you go last night? I came back from the phone and you were gone. I was worried about you." He shifted his briefcase to his other hand and looked at her expectantly.

"I'm sorry, Steven. I . . . It's too complicate to explain." *She* didn't understand her relationship with Vince. How could she expect anyone else to?

"It had something to do with Danelli, didn't it?" His eyes narrowed. "I saw him at the restaurant."

Ginger looked at the ground, positive the pain was reflected in her eyes. "Yeah."

"Did he hurt you?"

"Yes. I mean no. Of course he didn't hurt me." At least not physically, but did injury from mere words count? "Look, I know I have a habit of saying this lately, but could we change the subject?"

"Yes, of course. Enough said. I know it's a sore subject. Hey, there's someone I want you to meet." He glanced around the crowded hallway. "There she is. Penny, over here." Waving one hand above his head like a man bringing in a plane, he caught the woman's attention.

A petite blond wearing a navy suit walked over and put her arms around Steven's waist. She would have been plain, but the love shining like a beacon in her eyes transformed her into a beautiful woman.

"Ginger, this is my fianceé, Penny. Penny, this is Ginger."

"So you're the one who's stolen Steven's heart." Ginger stuck out her hand.

Penny laughed. "Actually, I think it's the other way around. He's stolen my heart. I feel like I've known you forever. Steven talks about you all the time." What started out as a handshake quickly turned into a hug.

Ginger brushed at the tear hovering near the corner of her eye. She hoped they could be friends. When they pulled apart, Ginger was sure the smile on Penny's face mirrored the one on her own. "All right, let me see the ring," she demanded.

Penny lifted her hand. The diamond caught the overhead light and sent a rainbow of color dancing on the walls.

"Oh, my God," Ginger gasped at the remarkable stone. It had to be at least three carats. "It's absolutely beautiful. Isn't your hand tired? You need a sling for this rock. Congratulations." Kissing Penny's flushed cheek first, then Steven's, she said, "I'm happy for both of you."

"I'd love to go to lunch with you some time, Ginger. I'd like us to be friends. Steven speaks so highly of you."

After she dumped him, he still considered her a friend? Why couldn't Vince find it in his heart to be that forgiving? "I would love to. The stories I could tell you about this guy. . . ." Ginger rolled her eyes.

"Hey! Don't give away my secrets. Not that I have many, but let her find out my faults on her own." The couple exchanged a loving glance as if they thought each other nothing less than perfect. "We can talk later," Steven said. "Right now we need to get inside before the trial starts."

"I'll be there in a minute. I need to visit the ladies' room." Ginger smiled after the pair until they disappeared behind the courtroom doors. The crowd in the hall thinned out until Ginger suddenly saw Vince staring at her, a troubled look burning deep in his eyes, a frown puckering his brow. The smile disappeared from her face. Her heart beat like a wild animal on the loose in her chest.

He took a hesitant step forward, and stopped. Ginger wondered if he realized what he'd seen was a continuation of the celebration he'd interrupted last night, and not the sordid affair he assumed it was. Why did he always have to think the worst of her?

Proving him wrong would hold no consolation. Ginger turned her back on him and walked away. He'd been dead wrong in treating her the way he had. Even if he never said it, let him choke on his own apology. Stubborn pride kept her from finding the words to forgive him.

"My complete name is Robyn Marie Jeffries. And before you ask, 'cause I know you will, Mr. Michaels, yes, I've gone by another name. That name is Robyn Banks. I used it in Steamboat. No, I didn't have any ulterior motives, I didn't know Vince Danelli, and I didn't steal anything out of his office." Robyn sat up straight in the witness chair, a satisfied smile stretched across her face.

Ginger winced and exchanged a worried glance with Steven. She couldn't help but wonder if Robyn's unusual style of testifying would hurt or help her case.

"Well, thank you very much, Ms. Jeffries, for attempting to do my job for me." A bemused expression flashed across David Michaels's face as if he'd never come across anyone quite like Robyn before. "Before you exonerate yourself and step off the stand, do you mind if I ask you a few more questions?"

"Shoot, counselor."

"Out of curiosity, is your assumed name an indication of your criminal tendencies?"

"No. Just my sense of humor."

"I see."

Ginger didn't think he believed it. From where she sat, they looked guilty.

"Where were you on the night of December ninth?"

"I was with my boyfriend at the Broadmoor in Colorado Springs. We had a romantic weekend, if you know what I mean." Robyn gave the lawyer a saucy wink.

The crowd roared with laughter.

David Michaels blushed. Ginger dropped her forehead in her hands and groaned.

"Spare me the intimate details," the prosecutor begged, placing both hands up to stop her flow of words. "Tell us, who did you leave in charge of your janitorial business in your absence?"

"Ginger," Robyn said.

"And you feel she is someone you can trust?" The lawyer's bushy eyebrows raised over eyes filled with skepticism.

Ginger held her breath, not sure what her own answer would be if their positions had been reversed.

Robyn scowled. "With my life, buddy." She smiled at Ginger.

Ginger smiled back with relief.

"What about the rest of your employees? Do you trust them?"

"I do a thorough background investigation on each and every new employee. They have all been with me for quite some time. I have no reason to suspect a single one of any wrongdoing. I trust them implicitly."

While the lawyer questioned Robyn further, Ginger hazarded a sidelong peek at Vince. Her glance caught his and she hastily looked away. Why was he staring at her? She fidgeted in her seat, uncomfortably aware that he was studying her every move. Trying to ignore Vince's presence, Ginger concentrated on Robyn's testimony.

"Do you always carry a pen with disappearing ink in your purse?" Michaels asked.

"Yes, I do. Every woman should. Sometimes it can be helpful."

"Could you be more specific?"

"You meet a guy you're not sure about, but you could get interested."

"Yes?"

"Well, you just write your number down with disappearing ink, and he thinks he's struck gold. You're off the hook if it turns out that you don't like him after all. Only it backfired in Steamboat. Heck, we didn't know until the other day Ginger used that very pen to write down her number for Vince. I mean, what are the odds?"

Robyn shifted her gaze to Vince and directed the rest of her speech toward him. "Actually, it was quite a revelation. It explains why she never heard from you, Vince. God, she was devastated when you didn't call. I didn't think she'd ever recover. She knew something had to be wrong, but she didn't know what. I was convinced you were hit by a beer truck or something."

Mortified, Ginger slunk lower in her seat, refusing to look at anyone, especially Vince.

"When Ginger saw you in the office building, she couldn't believe it. She almost had a heart attack."

Michaels pounced on the tidbit of information Robyn unwittingly gave out. "She saw him? Are you talking about the night of December ninth?"

Robyn's head swiveled around and she looked at the lawyer with blank eyes as if she'd forgotten he was there. "Is there another night in question here?"

The lawyer turned and pierced Ginger with his gaze. Heat flooded her cheeks. This guy had a way about him that would make even Sister Theresa feel guilty. Then he turned his head and leveled what Ginger was sure was his best you're-nothing-better-than-a-bug-under-a-microscope look on Robyn.

"Ms. Thompson saw my client, Vince Danelli, and didn't announce her presence? Don't you find that odd for someone who claims to be so in love with the man?"

"It's not a claim. She is in love with him. I don't find it odd behavior for a woman at all," Robyn defended.

"Come now, Ms. Jeffries, she hadn't seen or heard from him in what, two weeks? And yet, when she does, she hides? One has to wonder what Ms. Thompson was really hiding from." A dramatic pause filled the courtroom, then he continued. "Let me run my theory by you and you tell me if I'm right." David Michaels leaned one elbow on the witness stand and crossed his right ankle over his left.

Ginger longed to trip him or stick her

tongue out at him. Anything to shake his lawyerly arrogance.

"On the night of December ninth, you went to Colorado Springs with your boyfriend, which gives you an airtight alibi. You have Ms. Thompson take over in your place. She didn't expect to see Vince Danelli because he wasn't due in the office until the following week. When she did see him she realized the danger of her losing her cover so she hid. Isn't that how it really happened?"

"Interesting theory, counselor." Robyn leaned closer to the attorney. "The truth of the matter is Mr. Danelli never called Ginger, after promising her he would." She shot a dirty look in Vince's direction. "Ginger thought she'd been just another one-night stand to him. She was angry, hurt and humiliated. Justifiably so. When she saw him, it only intensified all those emotions.

"She did what any normal woman would have done, and ducked around a corner to compose herself. Besides that," Robyn added, "she was dressed in baggy sweats. What self-respecting woman would want the man she loves and hasn't seen in weeks to see her in grungy clothes? A woman has her pride, you know."

After filling two bowls to overflowing with chocolate ice cream, Ginger added whipped cream, nuts, and a cherry to each. Public humiliation was hard enough to swallow, but it would go down more easily with the help of this gooey concoction. She carried the bowls into her living room.

"For the hundredth time, I'm sorry, Ginger. Sometimes my mouth works faster than my brain." Robyn, sitting cross-legged on the sofa, took the bowl from her and dug her spoon in. She spoke between mouthfuls, "I think everything went our way today, don't you?"

Ginger grimaced. "Like Steven said, all we can do is tell the truth. Which reminds me, something's been bothering me since this afternoon. You said on the stand all your employees had been with you for a long time."

"They have."

"The guy I talked to said he'd only been working with you for a little while."

"What guy?"

Ginger took a bite of her ice cream and let the chocolatey comfort slide down her throat. "The one you hired last December."

Robyn paused with the spoon halfway to

her mouth. "I haven't hired anyone in over a year."

"Yes, you have. What did he say his name was?" Ginger tilted her head back and looked at the ceiling as if the answer was written there. "John something or other . . . John . . . John Johnson. That's it!"

"I've never heard of a John Johnson." Robyn turned brown eyes filled with apprehension toward Ginger.

Setting her half-eaten dessert on the glass-top coffee table, Ginger rose and paced across the room, then came back. "You have to have heard of him."

"Haven't."

"Say you have," she pleaded, twisting her hands together.

"Can't and won't, but tell me why."

"Because." Guilt flooded through Ginger like a dam bursting free of its walls. She closed her eyes, wishing in vain that she could change the past. "I gave him the keys to Vince's office," she whispered, opening her eyes again.

"You did what?" Robyn stood up from the sofa, her bowl of ice cream clutched in a white-knuckled grip.

"I gave him the keys."

Furiously, Robyn shoveled spoon after spoon of chocolate into her mouth.

Ginger walked over, tore the bowl out of her friend's steely grasp and set it on the table next to hers.

"Hey, I can handle my chocolate," Robyn cried in annoyance. "Why didn't you tell me all this before?" she asked, already forgetting the melting ice cream.

"He's one of your employees," Ginger insisted. "You said yourself you trusted them. Besides, I gave him keys to the office, not the safe."

"Safecrackers don't need keys. Why did you let this John guy in there anyway?"

"Because I'm an idiot!"

"Give me something besides the obvious to go on here."

Hurt, but knowing she deserved it, Ginger quickly rose and paced the floor again. "I guess I panicked. The thought of going into Vince's office scared the hell out of me. It would have been full of reminders of him, his belongings, his world, his life. Besides, I didn't want to find a picture of his latest girlfriend beaming up at me from the corner of his desk. You can understand that, can't you?"

Robyn rolled her eyes.

Ginger groaned. "Oh, wipe the smirk off your face. You would have done the same thing and you know it." She searched

Robyn's eyes, begging for some understanding of what she'd done. "When this guy offered to clean for me, I just said yes without really thinking."

"Even though I didn't hire him," Robyn mused.

"How was I to know?"

"You understand what this means, don't you?"

Ginger knew there was only one logical answer. "We were framed."

"You got it." Robyn ran her fingers through her hair. "This is better than a late-night movie. Only it would be much more entertaining if it was happening to someone else." She strode across the room and placed her hands on Ginger's shoulders, giving her a gentle shake. "We gotta nail these bastards. Do you think you can identify the guy?"

Ginger closed her eyes and fought to remember. "Probably. Average looking. No notable features. But I do remember what he looked like."

"Good. Let's get in the car and hightail it over to the police station. You're going to look through every mug book until we find him. Even if it takes all night."

Grabbing their purses, they raced out the door and jumped into Robyn's car. After a few blocks Ginger noticed Robyn casting worried glances in the rearview mirror. She reached forward and switched off the radio. "What's wrong?"

"Believe it or not, someone's on our tail."

Ginger's stomach plunged. "We're being followed?" Fear made her voice squeak. With a nervous glance, she peered out the back window. The lights from the car behind them momentarily blinded her.

"Bingo."

"What are we gonna do?"

Cranking the steering wheel hard to the left, Robyn took an unexpected sharp turn, sending Ginger flying against the door. She grabbed the arm rest, thankful she'd remembered to buckle her seatbelt.

"We lose 'em!"

"We were headed for the police station, for heaven's sake! Couldn't we just go to the police station?" Ginger, at that moment, would have given anything to have her ordinary, dull, boring life back. "Please! They have cops there and everything. They can help us."

"Quit panicking." Robyn made a quick right down an alley, left the smell of burning rubber on the street, and then made another left. "It's better to lose them. I've heard of people getting shot right in front of the cops."

At Robyn's words, Ginger sank lower in the seat, the image of bullets flying making her mouth unbearably dry. "Are they still back there?" she asked over the sound of squealing tires and the smell of burning rubber.

"Yeah. A couple more turns and I think we'll be home-free."

Ginger didn't have time to grab onto anything when the car took the next corner. The sharp right sent her careening into Robyn.

"Hey, I'm trying to drive here!"

Irritated, Ginger lashed out, "Watch it!"

"I am watching it. Pipe down." Robyn took her eyes off the road for a second to flash Ginger an indignant look.

Ginger growled in frustration and looked over her shoulder. The other car appeared to be farther away. "Just get us to the police station in one piece, okay?"

"That's the plan. Hold on!" Another sharp corner followed by a second sent them into an alley. Illuminated by the headlights of the car, a brick wall loomed in front of them.

Robyn slammed on the brakes just a few feet from impact. Ginger screamed and braced her hands against the dash. The car skidded to a stop. In jerky movements, Robyn shut off the lights and killed the ignition. The immediate stillness echoed with the sounds of their heavy breathing.

They glanced at one another, then in unison looked over their shoulders through the rear window. The other car flashed past the alley, its motor droning into the still night air.

"Do you think he spotted us?" Ginger asked, her eyes locked on the street behind them.

"It doesn't look like it. But let's just sit here for a few minutes anyway." Robyn heaved a sigh. "Was that wild or what?"

Turning her head, Ginger looked at her friend. The twinkle in Robyn's eyes was infectious. Now that the scare was over, Ginger had to admit it had been a little exciting. Her lips twitched and they both broke into giggles of relief at the same time. "Who do you think it was?"

"I don't know. Could your house be bugged? Maybe whoever it was knew we were going to look through mug books and wanted to stop us."

An involuntary tremor ran down Ginger's spine at the thought of someone in her home uninvited. The walls of the alley seemed to close in on her. She shivered. "Let's get out of here."

With a turn of the key, the car started up with a quiet hum. Robyn backed out of the alley in darkness. After making sure no one was around, she flicked the lights on. They completed the short drive to the station in silence. Robyn parked, then they went inside and explained their situation to the burly officer behind the front desk.

"Wait right here, ladies. I'll get the detective for you." He showed them to an office with short, partitioned walls.

"Do you think he'll believe us?" Ginger asked. Rubbing her temples, she sat down on the edge of a chair.

"I don't care if he does or doesn't. He can't stop us from looking at the mug books to see if we can find the creep that posed as one of my employees," Robyn whispered, plopping down in a chair next to Ginger.

"I hope this isn't going to take all night." Ginger tapped her fingers on the desk in front of her.

Beyond the door, keyboards clicked, phones rang, people shuffled in and out at a nonstop pace. God, the police station was a noisy place. Ginger's ears picked up on a conversation in progress.

"I knew I'd find you here." A man's voice

reached her ears. "I'm sorry, but I lost them. I was right on their tail but that one broad's a crazy driver. I lost them, Danelli."

As stunned as if she'd been punched in the face, Ginger looked at Robyn. Her friend's chin hung open in surprise.

They both mouthed the name "Danelli" at the same time.

There could only be one man with that name. Enough was enough. In unison, they leapt from their chairs and whirled around the corner.

Vince Danelli was standing in the next room. Ginger's eyes narrowed on him. "You had us followed?" she accused. Looking around, she had the satisfaction of seeing the startled look on his face before he managed to hide it. His fathomless green gaze unnerved her. As mad as she was, Ginger noticed how he looked. In jeans and a red T-shirt, he looked good enough to make her lose track of her thoughts. Almost.

"I don't believe you did it! How could you send this goon to follow us?" She gestured to the tall, skinny man standing silently next to Vince. With the coffee stain on his white shirt and the wrinkles in his pants, he looked like he'd been sitting in a car all day, no doubt watching her and Robyn's every move. "You scared the hell out of us." She shot the man a furious glare and turned back to Vince. "I thought we were going to be shot, for God's sake."

"I don't carry a gun, ma'am."

Ginger ignored him and kept her gaze on Vince. "What did you hope to discover by doing this?"

He looked ashamed. "I don't know," he said after a lengthy silence. "I really don't know anymore." His voice grew deep and husky, his gaze smoldering with an emotion that touched Ginger's soul. She noticed his hands clenching and unclenching at his sides.

"What are you doing here, anyway?" she asked, managing to find her voice.

After a slight hesitation, he answered. "Checking out the options for security at my office."

"I'm Detective Miller. What's going on here?" An officer came up behind them, stopping Ginger from finding an answer to his remark.

"Arrest these men," Robyn demanded, gesturing toward Vince and his friend.

The officer looked at her as if she'd lost her mind. "On what grounds?"

"On the grounds they've been harassing us." Robyn looked to Ginger for support.

Ginger and Vince continued to stare at each other, their gazes locked, contributing nothing to the conversation going on around them.

Ginger swallowed, her nerves getting the better of her, and tore her gaze away. She couldn't stand the haunting, tortured look she thought she'd seen in his eyes.

She didn't want to fight anymore. "Forget it, Robyn," she said. "They're just doing what we would under the same circumstances."

"But, Ginger, you're the one who —"

Ginger shook her head. "Forget it!"

"Fine." Robyn folded her arms across her chest and sniffed.

Ginger turned to the cop behind her. He was tall and slender and the crow's feet by his eyes indicated he knew a good joke when he heard one. The expression on his face held an understanding Ginger immediately related to. "Detective Miller, I understand you're familiar with our case?"

"Yes, I am."

"Good. Robyn and I have suspected all along we've been framed. We think we know one of the parties responsible. I'd like to look through your mug books to see if I can identify him." She could feel Vince move to stand behind her. The tantalizing male

174

scent of him combined with the heat from his body made her shift from one foot to the other trying not to acknowledge his undeniable presence.

"Who framed you?" His deep voice caressed her ear. "What's his name? Why didn't you tell me?"

Ginger edged away. "John Johnson," she answered. "But I think it's an alias. And I couldn't tell you because we're not exactly on speaking terms if you'll remember." She refused to turn around and look at him. She couldn't. She knew her emotions were prominently displayed on her face. Intense longing, hurt, betrayal. Despite what he thought she'd done, why did he have to hire a detective to follow her? It made her feel dirty and cheap. It made her feel like the crook he thought she was.

Tension hung in the air.

"The books, Detective?" Ginger reminded the officer.

"Yeah, right. Follow me to the Investigations Bureau." He led the way. Ginger and Robyn followed with Vince close on their heels.

"Why is *he* coming with us?" Robyn whispered in Ginger's ear.

"Because this involves me," Vince answered as if the question was directed at him.

He had every right to be there. Those architectural drawings had been stolen from *him*. He had every right to know who did it. Every right to be angry. Every right to hire a detective.

"Here you are." Miller waved a hand at the stacks and stacks of books lying on a table. "These are labeled by race, hair color, facial hair, etc. Pick out what you need. Happy hunting."

Grabbing a chair, Ginger plopped onto the seat and pulled the first volume toward her. "Make yourself comfortable, folks. This could take hours."

"Do you want some coffee?" Robyn asked.

A heavy breath escaped Ginger, ruffling the bangs above her eyes. She flipped the first page open. A dozen serious-faced men stared back at her. "Yeah. That would be great."

Two cups of coffee and three mug books later, Ginger's heart skipped a beat when Vince perched on the corner of the desk, his muscular thigh only inches away. She tried to concentrate on the criminals in front of her, but that masculine leg kept getting in the way. Vince swung the lower part of it back and forth like a pendulum. Ginger was hypnotized. How long had it been since she'd touched that leg, and run her hands up and down it?

To get a better look at the photos, Vince leaned toward Ginger, scattering her thoughts.

"Do you have to sit there?" she shot at him, irritated by her reaction to his closeness, how good he smelled, how much she wanted to touch him.

He raised an eyebrow. "Sorry." Sliding off the desk, he sauntered over to another chair and sat down.

"Wow, he's not bad-looking," Robyn peered over Ginger's shoulder and pointed to one of the photographs.

"For God's sake, Robyn. He's a convict."

"I don't want to date him. I'm just . . . window-shopping."

Irritated, Ginger accidentally knocked her coffee cup over spilling brown liquid all over the book. Grabbing a tissue out of her purse, she dabbed at the mess she'd made. She shoved her styrofoam cup in Robyn's hand. "Get me another cup of coffee, would you?" she growled.

"Sure."

Wiping up the last of the puddle, Ginger was convinced she'd never find the mysterious John Johnson. Frustrated, she grabbed the next book and opened it. Two pages in,

one of the faces drew her attention. She'd
seen this man before. It wasn't the guy
called John Johnson. It was someone else . . .
someone very familiar. "Oh, my God."

Chapter 9

Vince jumped up and stood at her elbow. "What? Did you find him?"

Jabbing her finger in the book, Ginger looked up at him. "Do you remember this guy?" she asked.

He placed one of his hands on the back of her chair and bent down.

"He looks familiar, but I can't place him." He looked from the book to her eyes.

Only inches from him, Ginger had to get up from her chair and move away. His closeness was suffocating. She couldn't think, or breathe.

Robyn walked in, coffee in hand. "What am I missing?" she asked, looking back and forth from Ginger to Vince, a puzzled look washing across her face.

God, how could she tell her this? "Robyn, are you still dating Rick?"

"Sort of. Lately his attitude has been colder than the other side of a pillow, though. Why do you ask?" Her eyes narrowed. "What does Rick have to do with any of this?"

Without a word, Ginger turned toward the mug book and pointed to Rick's picture.

Robyn took a hesitant step forward. Looking at the photo, an almost inaudible gasp escaped her lips. Her face paled. "I sure know how to pick them, don't I?" She smiled, but pain reflected deep in her brown eyes.

"I'm sorry, Robyn." Ginger placed a hand on her friend's arm, offering support.

"Where *have* I seen him before?" Vince asked.

Glancing over her shoulder, Ginger answered. "In Steamboat. We met him on our skiing trip. Don't you remember? He was going to have lunch with us. It makes sense now. When he saw you, Vince, he refused to come to the table."

A frown appeared on his face. "How do you know my presence is what kept him away?"

"Yeah," Robyn chimed in. "Rick said he didn't want to share me with anyone. He wanted me all to himself. He's not involved in this. He can't be. He can't be." Her voice had lowered to a quiet plea.

Ginger looked at the ceiling for guidance and dragged a hand through her hair. "Come on, you guys. Look at the facts. Robyn won free tickets to Steamboat.

Vince, you won free tickets to Steamboat. Your safe gets robbed. Robyn's company gets accused of that theft. A guy Robyn met, in Steamboat, shows up in a mug book. How many coincidences do you two need before the truth smacks you in the face?"

Robyn cleared her throat. "So what you're saying is Rick wasn't dating me because I'm a gorgeous brunette with a great body. He was dating me to get his hands on Danelli's damn designs?"

Ginger hung her head and stared at the floor. She didn't want to look up. She didn't want to see the hurt in her friend's eyes. A lump formed in her throat. Emotional pain took a long time to heal. She knew that better than anyone.

"Any luck yet?" Detective Miller walked through the doorway.

When no one answered, Ginger turned toward the officer. "We think so, but it's not who we were looking for." She showed him the photo of Rick.

Miller grabbed a pencil from behind his ear and jotted some notes down on a legal pad. "Let me look some info up on the computer. I'll be right back."

Ginger glanced toward Vince. He stood with his back to her, staring out the window into the black night. Her heart plummeted.

He still didn't believe her. Even with the evidence right in front of them, he still thought she was a crook.

The ten longest minutes of her life passed in silence. Vince never turned from the window. His jaw, in profile, was set in a rigid line.

The detective walked back into the room. "It seems Rick Dugan, aka Rick Flanders, aka Richard Milman, has quite a record," he announced.

"The bastard!" Robyn stood with her hands clenched at her sides, her eyes fury. "I'm going to rip his fat head off of his fat neck and feed it to the pigeons on the Sixteenth Street Mall."

Robyn made a beeline for the exit, but the detective stood in the middle of the doorway, effectively blocking Robyn's path. "Where do you think you're going, ma'am?"

"I'm going over to Rick Dugan Milman Flanders's house to get even for all the crap he's put me through."

The cop didn't budge an inch. If anything, he seemed to fill up more of the doorway. "This is a matter for the police. Just tell us his last known address and we'll handle the situation." He spoke in a calm, soothing voice as if trying to placate a crazy woman.

And Robyn was crazed. She stood with

her hands crossed over her chest in a manner that mimicked the man standing in front of her. A wicked smile danced on her lips. "I won't tell you, but I'd certainly be glad to show you."

"Sorry. The man has a known reputation for violence. We can't allow a civilian into a potentially dangerous situation."

"Officer, don't make me call you names," Robyn huffed.

"Lady, don't make me handcuff you to a chair." His eyes narrowed to tiny slits. Robyn was in over her head.

Ginger knew the situation was heading dangerously out of control. She had to do something. "Robyn, just tell Detective Miller Rick's address. Let him do his job," she pleaded.

Robyn shot her a dirty look, but Ginger held her ground. "The sooner you tell him, the sooner they can place the creep behind bars."

"Fine!" Robyn threw her hands up in the air in exasperation. Heaving a sigh, she scribbled the address on the notepad Ginger thrust into her hand and reluctantly gave it to the cop.

"Thanks. There's no sense in all of you hanging around. We'll call you after we've interrogated him if we have any questions we need answered." With a wave, he turned and left the room.

Robyn waited two seconds, and grabbed her purse off the desk. "Hurry up. We've got to get there before the cops do."

Shocked, Ginger grabbed Robyn's arm, stalling her. "What are you talking about? You can't be serious. You heard the officer. Rick could be dangerous."

"Oh, believe me, he can't be as dangerous as I feel right now." She yanked her arm free. "Are you coming, or aren't you?" she demanded, her eyes twin chips of ice.

Ginger stood rooted to the spot, debating whether she should stop Robyn or go with her.

"Fine. I'll go myself." Without waiting for an answer, Robyn whirled and stalked out of the room.

"Wait!" Ginger shouted. "Oh, God. What am I going to do now? I don't even have my car here." She turned and looked at Vince. She opened her mouth, ready to ask him to help her, then stopped. Look who she was asking! The man who thought she was a thief. And she wanted his help? Yeah, right. When pigs started flying.

Vince grabbed her elbow and pulled her from the room. "Come on," he muttered. "If we hurry, we can catch up to her."

Ginger looked up into his eyes, baffled at his change of attitude. "You'd do this for me? Why?"

When Vince stopped in his tracks, Ginger bumped into his back. She grabbed his arm to steady herself. His strength still had the power to unnerve her.

"Don't ask me questions I'm not going to answer." His green eyes blazed down at her with a look that melted her heart, then sent it into overdrive.

Flashing a hesitant smile, Ginger nodded. It was enough right now that he was willing to help. Wasn't it? "We'd better hurry," she reminded him when he stood there staring at her, a bemused expression on his face.

"Right." Vince took her hand in his. "Let's go."

Ginger gave Vince directions to Rick's apartment, then they both lapsed into a silence as thick as Denver's smog. Ginger was worried about Robyn.

An impending feeling of doom rolled through her body like thunder. What if Rick was a real nut case? What if he harmed her friend? What if the police arrived before they had time to yank Robyn out of the situation and they were all arrested for obstructing a police investigation?

"Drive faster," she urged Vince.

He obviously sensed the worry in her voice. Without even looking at her, he stepped down on the accelerator. She turned her head and studied his profile. God, she had missed being near him. He was so handsome, even with that serious expression. She missed his lone dimple. But it only appeared when he smiled. Lord only knew she hadn't seen him smile in a long time. Too long. It was as if their relationship had existed in another time and place — another world.

A slight frown creased his forehead. If she didn't know better she'd almost think he was worried about Robyn. Or maybe he was wondering why the hell he'd agreed to help her. The words formed on her lips to ask him why he had, but they pulled into the parking lot of the complex.

"Jesus. What does she think she's doing?" Vince said pulling the car to a screeching halt.

"What? Where?" Ginger scanned the area, spotting Rick and Robyn on the second floor landing. Before she even had time to open her door, Vince was out of the car and halfway up the stairs. Wrestling with her seatbelt in frustration when it wouldn't release, she yelled out "Wait for me!"

If Vince heard Ginger, he ignored her

plea. Finally rid of the belt, Ginger sprinted across the short expanse of grass and up the stairs. When she reached the top, she stopped short in her tracks. What she saw made her smile.

Robyn had the notorious Rick Dugan-Flanders-Milman, or whatever his real name was, pressed up against a wall. Sweat beaded on his brow, dampening an unruly lock of brown hair on his forehead.

"How dare you do this to me? How dare you? Just who do you think you are? I want to know who you work for, buster, and I want to know right now, or else!" Robyn shouted, waving a finger in the man's ashen face.

"I don't know what you're talking about. Is this because I don't want to go out with you anymore?" He started to move forward and Robyn pushed on his chest with both hands, effectively pinning him against the wall. The man was twice as big as Robyn. If he wanted to exert force, he could snap her like a twig.

Ginger leaned against the opposite wall next to Vince. "We need to get Robyn out of here," she whispered to him, "before he hurts her or the cops get here and arrest her."

He grinned at Ginger and her heart

lunged at the sight of his dimple. "In a minute. Let her vent her frustration."

"Listen, Robyn, what we had was . . . nice, but it's over. Finished."

"I'll let you know when I'm finished with you, you dirt bag." Robyn punched her ex-boyfriend in the gut with her knotted fist, forcing a whoosh of air from his lungs.

Rick doubled over, his arms protecting his stomach.

"Why did you do this to me?" Robyn demanded. "Why did you use my company as a cover? What did I ever do to you? I'm going to ask you once more who you work for, then I'm going to sic this big, burly guy on you." Robyn pointed to Vince.

Vince waved at Rick.

"Fess up! I know you couldn't have done this on your own. You're not smart enough." She grabbed a fistful of hair and yanked his head up.

Seizing her arm, Rick twisted it until Robyn dropped to her knees in pain.

"Ouch! You're hurting me," she cried out.

Vince stepped forward. "Nothing would make me happier than to take you apart inch by inch," he said, his voice deceptively soft. "Don't give me an excuse."

The wanted man dropped Robyn's arm as if it burned his flesh, fear shadowing his eyes.

Ginger heard the distant sound of sirens approaching. Tentatively, she touched Vince's arm. His skin was warm, his muscles rock hard. "Guys, we have to get out of here now."

"We can't," Vince said, not taking his eyes off Rick. "If we leave, he'll ditch the cops. I want to see this guy put behind bars where he belongs. I also need to know who his boss is. The cops will get it out of him . . . one way or another." Rick blanched.

"Give me five more minutes with him," Robyn said, rubbing her arm. She moved next to Ginger, safely out of harm's way. "I'll get all the information we need."

A crowd had gathered on the landing, obviously bored with the lack of action at the apartment hot tub. "You tell him, honey," someone called out.

"Ooooh, you really scare me, Robyn," Rick mocked. As if pairing off in their respective corners, the two circled each other until Vince effectively put a hand up against each, holding them apart.

Sirens wailing, two cop cars pulled into the lot, their flashing lights a stark brilliance in the darkness.

Ginger heaved a sigh of relief as well as guilt and yanked on Robyn's arm. They had been specifically ordered not to go to Rick's apartment. Maybe if they mingled with the crowd, Detective Miller wouldn't notice they were there.

Robyn shook off her grip and shot her a dirty look. "Stop it, Ginger. I'm not leaving."

A wild look flashed in Rick's eyes and in a burst of motion, he rushed forward and headed for the crowd to lose himself. Acting on impulse, Ginger stuck her foot out. Rick tripped over her leg and went sprawling on the ground.

Vince grabbed his arm and pinned it behind his back, holding him in place. He flashed a wicked grin up at Ginger. "Nice work."

She smiled back, her heart threatening to burst from his words. All it took was a simple compliment to make her knees go weak. "Thanks. Just doing my job."

The cops were already racing up the stairs, Miller in the lead. His disapproving gaze locked with Ginger's a second before moving to the man lying face down on the cement.

The ominous click of handcuffs rang out as Miller changed places with Vince. "We've been looking for you for a long time," he said, yanking Rick to a standing position. Shoving him against the wall, he frisked him. "Put him in the squad car. And don't forget to read him his rights."

Rick uttered a string of colorful oaths as the other officer led him none too gently down the stairs.

"You jerk," Robyn shouted at his retreating back. "I hope they give you life."

The glance Rick threw over his shoulder made Ginger shiver. They were lucky, damn lucky, he hadn't done anything to harm them. The guy was worse than dangerous.

"Nobody is getting any information out of me. Do you hear me? Nobody. Not a word. Not a single frickin' word." The officer yanked on his arm and Rick laughed. "I'll be out on bail in a couple of hours. Then I'm gonna come looking for you, pretty baby." He pursed his lips and kissed the air in Robyn's direction.

"Try it, buddy." Robyn's face paled, but she raised a fist into the air and shook it, refusing to let him know his words frightened her. "I'll be waiting."

Detective Miller came up behind them. "What are you people doing here when I specifically told you I didn't want you anywhere near this situation?"

"Seeking justice," Robyn fumed.

The cop shot her a disgusted look, then rolled his eyes. "Lady, your kind of justice usually ends up getting people killed." He held up a gun that he'd just confiscated from Rick. The squad car's lights flashed in the cold steel.

"Oh, God," Robyn sobbed, her face draining of all color. "I'm sorry." She placed one shaking hand over her mouth. "I'm sorry. I . . . I have to get out of here." She rushed down the stairs.

The detective looked at Ginger, one eyebrow raised in puzzlement.

"She was . . . fond of him." Ginger answered his unasked question. "It's kind of hard to discover someone you care about is not who you believed them to be." Vince stared at her, a questioning look in his eyes. Ginger looked away.

After an uncomfortable moment of silence, Vince turned to the detective. "Rick knows who's responsible for this whole mess," he said.

Miller nodded acknowledgment.

"What are you going to do about it?" Vince stood with his hands on his hips, his feet braced wide. Anger emanated from every pore.

A hint of a smile appeared at the corners of the officer's mouth. "We'll take the appropriate measures," he reassured them. "We'll interrogate him. As soon as we know

anything, you'll be the first person we call."
He turned to walk down the stairs. "If you'll
excuse me, I have to book a prisoner."

In about two seconds, Ginger would be
alone with Vince. An inner trembling
warned her it was a situation she didn't want
to find herself in. Not now. Not when her
emotions were so raw. "Detective, my ride
kinda left. Is there any way one of your offi-
cers can give me a lift?"

"We have to get back to the station with
our prisoner. Can I call you a cab, Miss
Thompson?"

"Don't bother," Vince spoke behind her,
his voice resonating with a clearness indicating he knew exactly what he was saying.
"I'll take her home."

He stood at the back of the crowd, watching Rick's arrest unfold before him. He was
so close. So close to throwing Danelli out of
the architectural industry. So close to removing the man from his mind and his
haunted memories.

Renard Duchaine absently rubbed the
five o'clock shadow on his chin. He'd in-
vested too much time and too much money
to be stopped at this point.

His eyes narrowed on Vince Danelli. He
looked invincible. But Renard knew better.

He'd been brought to his knees once. Vince's ex-wife had been so easy to manipulate. All he'd had to do was dangle money in front of her pert little nose and she'd done whatever Renard asked. Renard had known Liz better than her own husband had.

It didn't matter that the bitch had been *his* once. It didn't matter that Vince had stolen her away from him. Oh, he pretended he was asking Renard's permission. But Vince always took what he wanted. All the way back to grade school, Vince took what he thought should be his. Renard tried to block out the image of his parents, but the stirring of memories made them come down like an avalanche of unwanted feelings.

Why can't you be more like Vince? He's so smart. So kind. He is so nice and polite to us. Why can't you be more respectful? We are your parents, after all. In truth, Renard was an outsider in his own family. Vince was more like their cherished son than he could ever be. After a while, he'd stopped trying. It never would have mattered anyway. Renard could have handed them the world and Vince still would have been a better son in their eyes.

He hadn't talked to his parents in over ten years. He didn't miss them. He didn't need their love. He didn't need anybody. And

194

that included Liz. He never really loved her. It rankled him that Vince could steal her away. Just like he'd stolen his parents away. But he had the last laugh. He stole Liz right back. Even if he had to bribe her.

Danelli had fooled him, though. Instead of floundering in heartbreak and despair, he'd come back even stronger, his designs more elaborate and intricate than before. No one would ever take Renard Duchaine's designs seriously as long as Vince was in the picture.

The only course open to him was to take Vince Danelli out of the picture.

Once and for all.

Chapter 10

The moon spilled soft light into the interior of Vince's car, casting a bluish glow around Ginger. She sat with her hands in her lap, staring straight ahead. She looked nervous. Hell, he was nervous. Why did he offer to drive her home? Was he destined to forever fall for women who would rather betray him than stand by his side?

Vince wanted to turn in his seat and study her angelic face. But, he reminded himself, angry for his momentary weakness, it was just a trick of the light. Beauty and betrayal often went hand in hand.

What on earth had possessed him to offer Ginger a ride home anyway? he asked himself again. He couldn't see enough of the woman. Just one more look, he'd tell himself. Just one more and then he'd quit. Every chance he got he devoured her with his eyes. In the courtroom. In the police station. In his mind when he tried to sleep at night.

Ginger heaved a deep sigh that tore through his heart, and Vince's gaze went straight to her mouth, moist and illuminated by the moonlight. It was as if she'd just licked her lips. Or she'd just been kissed.

He gripped the steering wheel so tight, he thought it would crumble in his hands. A groan settled deep in his throat. Why, he asked himself for the hundredth time, why did she have this power over him? He wanted Ginger. Hell, he needed her with an intensity that rocked his whole body like an 8.5 on the Richter Scale. With his foot on the brake, Vince stopped at a red light.

"Thanks for the ride." Her voice, a seductive whisper to his ears, drifted across the interior of the car and tantalized his senses.

"No problem," he growled. *Like hell it isn't. How am I supposed to handle sitting next to you in my car? Your thigh is so close I could touch it, slide my hand up and down the length of your satiny skin.*

A car honked behind them. "The light's green," Ginger announced.

With a heavy foot, Vince stomped on the accelerator. The tires squealed in protest. Embarrassed, he eased up on the gas. He was acting like a highschool kid. As much as he wanted it, driving like a maniac would not steer thoughts of Ginger from his mind, or his need for her from his body.

197

Finally, when he was of the firm opinion he could take no more, they arrived at her house. Pulling up to the curb, Vince killed the engine. He turned his head and scanned her profile. "Do you mind if I come in?" he asked.

She cast a startled look in his direction.

"Why would you want to come in?" She tucked a strand of blond hair behind her ear with a shaky hand.

"We need to talk."

"I . . . I don't think so. I don't want you in my house. Not after the last time. We both ended up saying vicious things."

The *last time* he'd kissed her. Even in the darkness of the car, Vince could see the blush creep across her pale cheeks. "Fine. We'll stay right here and talk." He turned sideways on the seat and faced her.

"What do you want to talk about?"

"Trust." He could see her back grow rigid against the white leather seat.

"You've already told me you don't trust me, that you despise me, and you wish you'd never met me." She turned and looked him in the eye. "Are you out to rub a little more salt into the wound?"

He could see the hurt reflected in her blue gaze, but continued anyway, undaunted. "God, I want to trust you, Ginger. But I can't." Vince ran shaky fingers through his hair. *I won't allow myself to.*

She reached for the door handle.

Grabbing her arm he stopped her. "Don't you want to hear why?"

"Would it make a difference?" Her eyes sparkled angrily.

Vince tightened his grip. Touching her was torture, but he couldn't let her get away. Not until she understood. "Please?" He didn't know why he needed to explain. But dammit, he did.

"Fine," she mumbled, releasing the handle.

Reluctantly, Vince relaxed his fingers. Her skin looked pearly in the moonlight. He longed to brush his hand against the softness of her cheek. He wasn't supposed to feel this way for a woman who'd betrayed him. Muttering a muffled curse, he pounded his hand against the steering wheel in a fit of frustration. The sound of the horn reverberated through the still night air making them both jump. "There's something I have to do before we talk." Vince watched her swallow nervously.

"What is it?"

"Kiss you." His gaze locked with Ginger's. Her pupils dilated, but because of surprise, elation, or fear he wasn't quite sure. His hand reached across the short expanse between them. With a tender touch, he tucked a wayward curl behind her ear, and slipped his fingers around the soft nape of her neck to draw her toward him. God, this felt so right, so good. This couldn't be a woman he had to fight like hell to resist.

She didn't oppose him, but she didn't help.

"Why are you doing this?" Ginger asked, her voice a husky whisper which only sharpened his craving.

"Because I *need* to."

"You can't trust me, yet you want to kiss me?"

He lowered his head to nuzzle the base of her creamy throat. "Damned if I can figure it out myself."

Vince's words echoed through her mind, leaving Ginger with an aching knot in her stomach. "Maybe *I* don't need to kiss someone who doesn't *trust* me." With strong hands, she pushed at his chest. How easy it would be to pull herself against him, curl into his warm embrace, satisfy her long-denied hunger for the man. But she wouldn't be a one-night stand to anyone, ever again. Least of all him.

With a flip of the handle, the door flew open and Ginger nearly fell out in her haste to get away. She ran up the sidewalk, fumbling in her purse for her keys.

"Ginger, wait!"

Trying to unlock the door and choke back her sobs at the same time proved too much for her. Her trembling fingers dropped the key ring. It hit the brick walk with a jangle. "Damn. Why now?" she mumbled with tears blurring her eyes. She couldn't even see to pick them up.

A warm masculine hand grabbed her arm and swung her around. Her back pressed against the rigid door while she faced the equally immovable Vince Danelli.

"I don't know why you affect me the way you do." His breath stirred the hair at her temple.

Ginger fought back a nearly irresistible urge to throw herself into his arms.

"I only know you do and I'm damned helpless to deny it. You can't lie to me. You feel it, too. I know you do. I see it in the way you look at me. I feel your body tremble when I'm near you. It's happening right now. Can't you sense the electricity between us?" Vince ran his hands up and down her arms, and traced a finger across the mound of one breast.

A shiver slid its way down Ginger's spine. She closed her eyes, and bit her lip. Forcing herself, she fought the quiver racing through her body at his simple touch. No, she couldn't lie to him. Not intentionally. She licked her lips. "So what if I feel it? It doesn't mean anything." She tried to lace as much hate as she could into her voice, but it came out sounding like a seductive whisper instead.

"Doesn't it?" Bending down, he picked up the key ring. Every muscular inch of his body pressed against hers. He shoved a key into the bolt and opened the door. "We can't fight it, so let's stop trying. I'm not good at playing games. Never have been." With ease born of strength, he picked her up in his arms. "Where's the bedroom?" he asked, slamming the door shut with his foot.

Ginger gazed into his green eyes, watched them darken with need. "I . . ." She wrapped her arms around his neck. "I can't do this, Vince."

"Don't lie to me."

"Alright," she whispered, saying the words she'd longed to say for more months than she cared to count. "I want you. I want you so bad it hurts. I need to feel your body against mine. I need you in my bed. I long to have you inside me. Is that what you wanted to hear? Do you feel better now?"

"Not yet."

Against her chest, Ginger felt his heart beat in unison with hers. "Down the hall and to the left." Conceding defeat, she lay her head against his broad shoulder as he strode down the corridor to her bedroom. Why was she doing this? Why couldn't she say no? There was no hope that this would ever last. Making love with Vince would only cause her pain. Tomorrow she might hate herself for her weakness, but for now, longing took over where common sense left off.

Vince laid her on top of the white quilted coverlet and covered her body with his. Warm hands trapped either side of her face. "God, I want you, Ginger." Fully dressed, the ridge of his erection pressed against her, told her how very much he wanted her.

Ginger's heart beat in wild anticipation. She wanted him. She yearned for him. The here and now was the only thing that mattered. Tomorrow would come soon enough. Regrets could wait until then. "Then take me," she begged, her voice a breathless whisper, barely audible even to her own ears. But he heard her.

His lips descended. Slow and sure. Ginger closed her eyes and moaned deep in her throat. This was what she'd been waiting for. Vince's kiss made her feel whole. Alive.

Satisfied. She had to make this moment last a lifetime, 'cause it was the last one she'd have with him.

He dragged his lips from hers and found her breast. Through her cotton shirt, his teeth caught her nipple and teased it.

She groaned and arched against him, offering herself without inhibition. Intending to pull him closer, Ginger threaded her fingers through his hair. He discovered her mouth again and the kiss intensified. In a flurry of arms and legs, they helped each other shed unwanted clothes. The line Ginger had on any rational thought snapped when Vince rubbed his naked body against hers. Skin against skin. Need against need.

Hungry hands touching everywhere, made Ginger's world spiral out of control. She was ready. She needed him. "Now, Vince. I need you now." She nipped at his lips, wrapped her legs around his waist, opened herself to him. In a voice raw with passion, she urged him on, begging for the release only he could give. Vince drove into her and she cried out at the exquisite sensation.

"Sweet Jesus." Grabbing her hips, Vince rolled onto his back and pulled her on top of him. His hips pushed against hers. Ginger placed her hands on his chest, propping herself up, matching his erotic rhythm stroke for stroke. Driving against him, she gave of herself an intensity that almost frightened her.

From her hips, Vince's hands blazed a trail across her stomach to her breasts. When he gently squeezed the fullness of her taut nipples, her head rolled back with the sweet torture of it. Over and over, Ginger cried out his name and found her release at the same time Vince's body shuddered with his own.

Sliding into the embrace of his arms, she snuggled against his chest in the happy exhaustion of the afterglow. Vince kissed the top of her head and Ginger drifted into a world of euphoria with her eyes closed, sleep ready to overtake her. She loved this man. Forever.

Vince tensed, then untangled his legs from hers. Ginger's eyes opened, her heart thudding with dread in her chest. "Where are you going?" she asked when he sat on the edge of the bed and reached for his jeans. She licked lips suddenly gone dry.

Vince had never promised anything. He'd come right out and said he didn't trust her. He hadn't forced his way into her bed. She'd begged him to take her like a wanton whore.

Begged him with a force any sane man couldn't resist.

"You said you wanted to talk," Ginger reminded him, staring at his naked back. Her eyes filled with tears. Now was not the time for touching. Now was the time for "the morning after" even if night still blackened the sky.

Vince stood, pulled his jeans over lean hips and zipped them. Turning around, he let his gaze stroll all over her bare skin.

Ginger shivered. Suddenly self-conscious, she tugged at one corner of the quilt, pulling it around her body to hide her nakedness from his view. The nakedness his hands had caressed so lovingly. The nakedness she'd given to him so freely. Ginger sat on the edge of the bed, flushed and tousled, but feeling cold all over.

Walking over to the pale blue wingback chair across from the bed, Vince sat as if he hadn't a care in the world. As if their lovemaking had no effect on him, and he didn't need her for anything other than physical pleasure. Bare-chested, he still wore only his jeans. His red T-shirt lay in a tangle at her feet.

Ginger stared at the shadows dancing on the ceiling. "I feel like I've known you forever," she choked out, shifting her gaze to

206

his. "But right now I feel like I don't know you at all. Why, Vince? Why does it have to be this way?"

He didn't answer. He didn't have to. She knew the reason. They both knew the reason.

Her betrayal and her lies. Harmless little white lies that had changed the course of both of their lives for the worse.

Her vision had adjusted to the darkness well enough to see the creases appear on his forehead, his eyes widen in surprise. Vince could pretend he didn't care, but she knew he was as affected by what had just happened between them as she was. "I believe you wanted to talk about . . . trust."

Silence stretched into minutes, broken only by the clock ticking on the nightstand.

"I don't have a prayer when I'm around you," he whispered into the quiet night.

Her heart ached with an intensity that threatened to crush her ribs. "W-what do you mean?"

"After my divorce from Liz, I was so bitter. I could walk away from anyone — but I can't seem to walk away from you. The damned irony of it is that I can't seem to stay with you either. Trust. Without it, we have nothing. Without it, no matter how much I want you, no matter how good we are together . . . I can't stay."

Ginger wanted to unleash the white-hot tears pricking at her eyes, but forced herself not to. She had to hang on to some of her pride. "Someday, Vince Danelli, you'll realize you could have trusted me all along."

"I can't count on that."

Tears of frustration blurred her vision. She rapidly blinked to clear them away. "Why, Vince?"

He rose from the chair and padded barefoot to the window. Half turning toward her, he shoved his hands into his front pockets, his shoulders hunched as if protecting himself from some unseen pain.

He looked, for a moment, like a lost little boy. Ginger wanted to wrap her arms around him, hold his head against her breast and soothe him with gentle words of love. But she knew it was better to let him talk.

"I married Liz when we were both young and naive. I thought we had the kind of relationship that would last forever. Hell, we were the kind of couple who finished each other's sentences." He flashed Ginger a half smile that didn't reach his eyes and turned back to the window.

"I landed a job with a prestigious architectural firm right after college. They loved my designs. I was on top of the world. That's when my relationship with Liz began to crumble. But, like a fool, I ignored the signs." There was a hint of indifference in his laugh. "I tried to keep her love by buying her presents, the more expensive the better. Jewelry, cars, you name it. Soon it wasn't enough. She was spending more than I was making.

"Money got to her. God, it was like she was possessed. She became greedy. One night while I was sleeping she crept into my den and stole one of my designs. She sold it to a competitor. She didn't love me as much as the color of money. I loved Liz. I trusted her. She betrayed that trust."

Ginger's mouth opened in shock. How could someone do that to the man they loved? To Vince? She forced herself to remain seated. "I'm not Liz," Ginger reminded him.

"No, but you stand charged with the very same crime." He pierced her with an accusing stare.

Her chin lifted defiantly. "I'm innocent, Vince."

"I'd like to believe that more than anything in the world. But until the guilty party is revealed, I can't."

Ginger's heart shattered into a thousand

tiny pieces she wanted to sweep under the carpet and forget. But there was no such thing as forgetting where Vince was concerned. "When my innocence is proven — and believe me, it will be — what happens the next time, and the next? What if I come home late from work? What if, God forbid, you misplace one of your plans? Will I be the one you turn to time and time again to blame?" Ginger wrapped the quilt tighter around her, trying in vain to block out the hurt.

"And if it's not me, what about the woman after me, or the one after her? I pity anyone you end up with, Vince. She'll never meet your expectations, no matter how hard she tries. No matter how much she loves you or you love her. Trust," she paused, "works both ways." The thought of him with another woman sent a jolt of pain through Ginger that she couldn't entirely hide. "I think before you ever place your faith in a woman again, you'd better try and believe in yourself first." Miserable, Ginger drew a deep breath. "You'd better go." *Please, Vince, stay with me. Let's work this out. Let's try and salvage what we have left.*

The look Vince gave Ginger told her that her words had hit home. On bare feet he strode across the carpet. He stood in front of her, hands hanging limp at his sides — a look of defeat settling on his handsome features. He looked like he wanted to touch her, but he didn't. "I don't want this to be the end."

The ragged sound of his voice was almost her undoing. "How can it be the end when you refuse to ever let there be a beginning?"

A muscle pulsed in his jaw and Ginger longed to reach out and touch it. Touch him.

"Ginger, I —"

She tore her gaze from his. "Just go, Vince. Please." Her voice caught on a sob.

With a muffled curse, he snatched his discarded clothing off the floor and strode to the door. Pulling on his shirt, Vince turned and looked at her. "I want to believe you're innocent," he said in a harsh voice. "I want to trust you, but —"

"That's just it, Vince. There's always going to be a 'but,' isn't there?"

He shoved his feet into his shoes. "See you tomorrow at the courthouse." He turned and left.

Chapter 11

Filled with antiques and collectibles, Judge Winston's chambers radiated an ambience that was at once comfortable and friendly. But as cozy as the surroundings were, Ginger shifted uneasily in her chair. All parties involved with the court case had been summoned to meet in the judge's office. Vince had not yet arrived. He was the *last* person she wanted to see after last night.

"Quit fidgeting," Robyn insisted. "You're making me nervous." She leaned closer to peer into Ginger's face. "You look as bad as I feel."

"Gee, thanks," Ginger mumbled.

She knew there was no way out of her misery except to forget Vince. The man had no intentions of ever trusting *any* woman. Not now. Not ever. No one could ever hope to get through the rock-hard wall he'd built around himself.

The door opened and Ginger's spine stiffened. Steven breezed into the room and she expelled a puff of breath. God, she had to stay calm. She couldn't let Vince know just how much his presence affected her. She couldn't let herself know.

"Ladies," Steven said taking the empty seat on the opposite side of the oak conference table, excitement dancing in his eyes. "Rumor has it we may have a stay of execution."

Robyn leaned as far as she could across the oak table. "Spill it, counselor. I want details. What are you talking about?"

Ginger swallowed hard knowing his news must have something to do with the events of the previous evening and Rick's arrest.

"I'm not sure. We'll have to wait and see what the judge says," Steven replied.

The door opened again and Ginger took several deep breaths. Then she looked up, straight into Vince Danelli's eyes. Her heart thumped so loudly she thought for a desperate moment that everyone in the room could hear it. So much for staying calm.

He slipped into the chair on the far side of the table from Ginger, a wary look in his eyes. In his dark blue suit, Vince looked dignified and utterly sexy, as usual. Fiddling with the strap of her purse, Ginger glanced at him beneath her lashes. For the thousandth time she reminded herself of her mother's words. *A sexy man was a dangerous man.*

And Vince was the sexiest.

The most dangerous.

An irresistible man should be avoided at all costs.

From now on, Ginger vowed to do her best to evade him. If she'd only heeded her mother's advice, she could have saved herself a lot of heartache.

Damn him.

Didn't Vince know they were on opposite sides — sides that had nothing to do with courtrooms, and judges and lawyers — sides that dealt with words like commitment, love and trust? Why couldn't he give her a chance? But he had answered the question for her last night.

He had no confidence in women.

Ginger was a woman.

Therefore, they were enemies.

The door to the chamber opened yet a third time. Judge Winston strode in. Swishing her black robe aside, she took the chair at the head of the conference table with an air of elegant superiority. "Thank you all for joining me here today." The grey-haired woman opened the manila file before her and continued. "I'm waiting for a phone call for confirmation, but it seems as if your case has taken a drastic turn." Peering over the top of her bifocals, Judge Winston looked at everyone in the room one by one.

"Depending on the outcome of the call, we may have discovered the party responsible for the theft of Mr. Danelli's architectural designs."

The door opened and a bailiff entered. "Your honor, Detective Miller is on the line for you."

"Ah, this is what I've been waiting for. Please excuse me. I'll be right back."

Silence filled the room. Ginger closed her eyes and mentally counted the ticking seconds from the wooden clock displayed on the mantel.

"Great weather we're having, isn't it?" Robyn asked no one in particular. No one answered. "How about those Broncos?"

"For God's sake, Robyn," Steven said. "It's the middle of baseball season."

Ginger opened her eyes in time to see Steven's impatient frown.

"I'm just trying to make conversation. Geez."

Ginger's gaze shifted to Vince. He was looking straight at her, wearing a bored expression. Mr. Calm, Cool, and Collected. Resentment boiled inside her. How could he act like nothing had happened between them? She knew last night wasn't a dream. He'd kissed her the way women fantasize about being kissed. He'd made love to her like a man in love.

Ginger wanted to howl at the fate that had thrown her into such an impossible situation. Why had she fallen for a man who stood for everything she'd fought against her entire life? Why?

Studying the hard line of his jaw, the sensitive shape of his mouth, the sweep of jet black hair against his forehead, Ginger tried to find answers. Except for the obvious fact that he was about as handsome as a man could get, he kept his real self hidden. But Ginger could never forget the glimpse of the tender, thoughtful, funny, sensitive man that he really was, no matter how hard he tried to make her forget. No matter how hard she tried to make herself forget.

As unobtrusively as she'd exited, the judge reentered the room. It was a struggle, but Ginger wrenched her gaze from Vince's studied indifference.

"Mr. Danelli," Judge Winston directed her full attention at Vince. "It seems the man Detective Miller took into custody last night decided to plea bargain. He divulged the name of the person who'd hired him. Are you familiar with anyone by the name of Duchaine?"

"Renard Duchaine?" Vince asked, a look of disbelief jumping to his face.

The judge flipped open her file and nodded. "The one and only."

Ginger watched as Vince pushed away from the table and stood, his brows drawn together in concentration.

"Duchaine and I grew up together. His family was like my family. I think I spent more time at his house than my own. We were great friends until my designs started receiving more attention than his." Vince rubbed a hand over his chin. "I still don't know why, but he tried to turn my professors against me. When that didn't work, he tried to turn my bosses against me. When that failed, he managed to bribe my former wife." He turned and pierced Ginger with a look of pure hatred. "I'm surprised I didn't realize sooner you worked for the bastard."

Pushing her chair back, Ginger stood, her hands clenched at her sides, her fingernails digging painfully into her palms. "I don't know Renard Duchaine. I didn't steal your designs. I don't work for anyone who stole your designs." She swung her hand wide, her voice ringing louder and louder with each syllable. "I told you over and over again that I had nothing to do with *any* of this."

Ginger rounded the corner of the table and stalked toward Vince. "What do I have to do to convince you that I'm innocent?" she demanded, jabbing him in the chest with her index finger.

Vince stared at her impassively which only angered Ginger further. "Don't look at me like that," she shouted. "Get mad. Yell at me. Show some damn emotion for a change."

"Why?" he asked in an oddly calm voice.

Tears pricked at her eyes. "Because it proves you're alive."

His eyes narrowed. "Who the hell says I'm alive?"

"I do, damn you." Ginger pounded on the hard wall of his chest with her two clenched fists, furious with him, and oblivious to everyone else in the room. "I've seen the passion in you. Why are you doing this to us? Why are you pretending we don't exist? Why?"

"Ginger, knock it off," Steven warned.

"Get your client away from my client!" Vince's lawyer entered the fray.

"Do I have to call the bailiff?" the judge asked, authority filling her voice.

"You tell him, Ginger," Robyn threw in over the other voices.

A firm hand gripped her arm, but still seething with anger, Ginger shook it off. "What do I have to do," she demanded of Vince once more, "to prove to you I'm innocent? Throw down my life for you?" She laughed bitterly through her sobs. God, at this moment, she almost hated him. "*What do you want,* Vince? Just tell me what you want." Rivulets of tears streamed freely down her cheeks.

Vince appeared unshaken by her outpouring of emotion. "I don't want . . . anything . . . from you."

Ginger felt as if he'd plunged a knife into her chest. But after the pain came a merciful numbness.

"Come on, Ginger."

This time she didn't resist when Steven pulled her away from Vince. She couldn't. She had nothing left but regret.

"Your Honor, with your permission, I'd like to recess until another time," Steven threw over his shoulder as he walked Ginger to the door.

"I think that's a splendid idea. Permission granted. Call my office tomorrow. Right now it would be best if you got your client out of here."

Silently, Ginger followed Steven like a little lost sheep. She could hardly breathe and her voice shook when she spoke. "Where are you taking me?"

"Home."

"Let me go to the restroom first. I'd like to compose myself, splash water on my face." Ginger looked into Steven's concerned gaze. "Please?" she begged. "I'm fine, really."

"Alright, alright," he conceded. "Robyn, you go with her."

"I'm not a baby," Ginger sighed. "I can take care of myself."

"No one said you couldn't," Robyn added. "But I *have* to go, if you know what I mean. Too much coffee this morning, so you're going to have to put up with my company whether you like it or not."

The face looking back at Ginger from the restroom mirror didn't even resemble the woman she knew. Wet streaks down her cheeks provided evidence of her tears, her humiliation. Her eyes were red and swollen, her hair matted to her temples, her cheeks pale. She gave a vain attempt at a smile.

"You know, Ginger," Robyn said from one of the stalls. "What we need is a vacation."

Ginger couldn't help laughing. The harder she tried not to the harder she laughed. Holding her arms across her aching stomach,

Ginger managed to wheeze out, "That's what got us in this problem in the first place."

"I see nothing funny about my suggestion," Robyn said. Exiting the stall she stood in front of the mirror. "This, without a doubt, would have to be a man-free vacation. Just the two of us." She took a lipstick tube out of her purse and applied another layer of bright red across her lips.

The more Ginger thought about it, the more she liked the idea. "You know, I have some time off coming up. Let's get as far away as possible. I hear Vermont is beautiful this time of year."

Robyn shoved her lipstick back in her purse, fluffed her bangs, then stuck out her hand and shook Ginger's. "You're on, partner."

With a half-smile that masked her inner pain, Ginger followed Robyn out of the restroom. Steven stood in the hallway worry furrowing his brow.

"What was all that laughing going on in there? I was ready to risk my manly reputation and come in after you two."

"Well, counselor, if you must know, we were discussing the vacation we plan on taking," Robyn informed him.

He looked from Robyn to Ginger skeptically. "You have to be kidding!" He threw his hands up in the air. "Someone please tell me this is a joke."

"What's the matter with us wanting to get away?" Ginger asked, confused about why it should bother him.

"Ladies, this case isn't over. And neither of you is leaving this town until it is. Do you understand?" Pointing at them, he spoke as if he was talking to children, enunciating each and every word.

Robyn slapped him on the back. "Relax, counselor. We'll be patient and wait until they hang the bastard responsible for ruining both of our lives." She winked at him. "My woman's intuition has been itching all day. I have a feeling things are going to be breaking loose real soon."

"Well, I'm glad you're so confident," Steven shot back at her sarcastically.

"Come on, you two, I've had enough fighting for one day. I'd just like to go home and try to forget this morning ever happened," Ginger sighed.

At least Steven had the grace to look ashamed. "You're right." He pulled her arm into the crook of his elbow. "You're absolutely right. Let's get out of here."

A peculiar tightness surrounded Vince's chest when Ginger left the judge's chamber.

In a weird way, he admired her. No matter what she managed to stand tall.

Lord only knew Vince had had enough of the fighting, but he couldn't help himself. Ginger was his weakness. Fighting was the only thing he knew how to do to protect himself.

"I'll call the judge's office tomorrow and see when we reconvene." David Michaels, Vince's lawyer, stood at his elbow, a harsh reminder of where he was and what had just taken place.

How had he uttered those contemptible words? Why hadn't someone stopped him? Better yet, why couldn't he have stopped himself? How Ginger must detest him. Hell, Vince hated himself now far more than he'd ever hated Renard Duchaine. "Call me," was all he managed to say to his lawyer before he strode out the door.

The marble courthouse steps reflected the bright glare of the August day, momentarily dazzling him. Out of the corner of his eye, he saw Ginger walking through the doors. He wanted to go to her, but his feet seemed rooted to the spot.

She stood only yards away, blond hair shining in the sunlight, her face wearing the same miserable expression he carried in his heart.

Should he go to her?

Dare he even try?

He loved Ginger. He needed her in his life. Yet it was as if an invisible line separated them and he'd have to force himself to cross it. She'd tried to mend the rift between them. Now it was his turn. He started toward Ginger, her name on his lips.

"Danelli!"

Before he could say anything, someone shouted his name. Vince shielded his eyes with one hand against the sun. A flash of metal caught his eye before his vision adjusted to the harsh light.

Renard Duchaine stood at the bottom of the steps. He clenched the butt of a .357 magnum in his hands like a crazed man, the barrel pointed straight at Vince. "Say your prayers, Danelli. You won't best me ever again."

Sweat formed on Vince's brow, a trickle heading for his eye. He longed to swipe it with a hand. Reason told him not to move. Behind him, people buzzed with fear.

"Oh, my God, he's got a gun!" Scurrying feet echoed on the steps as people scattered.

Vince's mouth dried. "Be reasonable, Renard." He held a palm up in front of himself, fingers splayed wide in a vain attempt at protection. "Let's talk."

A demented look widened Duchaine's eyes and Vince watched the man's trigger finger tighten.

Death was close.

Vince could feel it. Taste it.

"Why? What have I ever done to you? I thought we were friends."

Duchaine blinked, licked his lips and shook his head. "No! You were never my friend. You took everything away from me. Everything. My parents. Liz. Any chance I ever had in the industry."

God, did he really believe Vince could have done all that to him? At one time they had been like brothers. "Your designs were good, Renard."

"But yours were always better, weren't they?" Duchaine laughed bitterly. "I won't allow it to happen again. Kiss it goodbye."

"No!"

Someone flew in front of him as a gunshot rang out, deafening him. Together they fell to the ground.

Vince looked up into Ginger's pale face.

"I'm sorry," she whispered before her eyes rolled back into her head, then closed.

A terrifying wetness seeped through his shirt. He looked down. "Jesus!" Crimson blood pooled around them. Stunned, Vince sat up and pulled Ginger into his arms, cradling her like a newborn baby.

He couldn't think.

He couldn't feel.

He just sat there rocking her back and forth.

Someone rushed to his side and shook his arm. Vince ignored the interruption and continued to gaze at Ginger's pale face.

"Snap out of it, Danelli!" Steven hovered over him, concern etched in his face. "The ambulance is on its way. Help me stop the bleeding!"

Vince's body jerked as if he'd been slapped. Jesus. He was sitting there letting Ginger die. Adrenaline surged. Ripping off his jacket, he pressed it to the wound on her chest. With shaky fingers he felt for the pulse in her neck. It was there. Weak, but there.

The garish red stain spread through his jacket. "Oh, God, why?" His heart pounded in his chest.

He'd never felt more helpless.

Or more hopeless.

Chaos continued to reign all around him. A quick glance over his shoulder reassured him Duchaine was handcuffed and had a half-dozen cops swarming around him.

Steven grabbed Ginger's wrist and looked

at his watch. "Where the hell is that ambulance?"

Throw down my life for you.

My life for you.

My life for you.

Vince pressed down harder on the wound to staunch the flow of blood as Ginger's words echoed in his head. Tears blurred his vision.

"Hold on, baby." He choked on the immovable lump in his throat. "Don't give up on me. Don't you dare give up on me."

Chapter 12

He didn't belong. Not here. The door closed behind Vince, effectively blocking out the sterile smell of antiseptic, the hospital staff rushing back and forth in green scrubs, and the squawking intercom demanding the immediate presence of a doctor in the ER. The heavy oak panel supported his weight as he leaned against it, refusing to move any further into the quiet room.

Candles twinkled and glistened inside the tiny hospital chapel. An unwelcome feeling of serenity invaded his body. Closing his eyes, Vince fought the sensation like a man fighting for his last breath. He didn't deserve serenity.

The image of Ginger, pale, fragile, connected to wires and tubes and machines that clicked and beeped and hummed sprang into his mind.

His chest constricted. Breathing hurt. Yet, Vince welcomed the pain, wished for it, instead of the calm emotion the chapel instilled in him.

He deserved anguish.

Suffering.

Torture.

He deserved to be lying in that hospital bed instead of Ginger. She was an innocent victim of circumstance. A victim of Renard Duchaine's bitter hatred and burning desire for revenge. Why couldn't Vince have seen the truth earlier?

He had not listened. He had only seen things the way he wanted to see them. Never had there been a person he could trust more in his life than Ginger. He knew that now. But knowing served no purpose. Because of him she'd been shot, and she was fighting for her life.

If she survived the night, it would be a miracle.

A miracle? What a joke. Vince swore under his breath. The image of Jesus seemed to gaze back at him. Sympathy and understanding radiated from the statue's marble eyes. Vince pushed his weary frame away from the door. He was doing this for Ginger, he reminded himself. Only Ginger. Not because God would intervene. If there was a God, and he had serious reservations, this whole travesty would have never happened.

Walking down the red-carpeted aisle,

Vince slid into the second pew. The first row wasn't reserved for sinners like him. He'd given up on religion and God and prayers long ago. God never listened anyway.

Awkward and unsure, Vince pulled himself forward onto the kneeler. He folded his hands together in prayer. He was a boy again — visiting church every Sunday with his parents — safe in the belief that God did exist and could fix anything.

Everything.

Dear God, save Ginger. If you do I promise to love and trust and protect her with my heart, my soul . . . my life. For whatever it's worth, I love her, God.

A hand clamped his shoulder. Vince jumped. His heart raced in his chest. He looked up into the wrinkled face of the man who'd startled him. "I didn't hear you come in, Father," he managed to whisper.

The priest flashed him a kind smile. "I'm sorry, my son. I'm Father O'Donnell. You looked distraught. I wondered if perhaps you needed somebody to talk to?"

Vince stared at the man, speechless, his mouth suddenly dry.

"I've been told I'm a good listener." The older man smiled kindly.

Vince's chest tightened, and he bowed his head wearily.

"I'm here for . . . someone I love very much. I'm here for her — nothing else." He looked around. "I haven't been in a church in years."

"Of course. I understand. That's true for a lot of the people who come into this chapel." The priest's unwavering blue gaze held Vince hypnotized. "But what you need is in your heart — in your ability to love and be loved. Trust in God, my son. The rest will follow." With another squeeze to his shoulder, the priest left as quietly as he'd appeared.

Vince hung his head in utter defeat. He'd worked hard to build a wall around himself, tall enough and strong enough to keep agony at bay. Or so he'd thought.

Ginger had chipped away at that wall inch by inch, layer by layer. And now, a total stranger, a man of the cloth, reminded him of a truth he had lost — the abiding power of love. A love she had freely given that he had refused out of fear.

He hung his head in shame, overwhelmed with emotion.

But if Ginger didn't make it . . . ? His heart thumped in his chest and almost stopped for a moment. How could he continue his life without her?

Trust in God.

Could it be that simple?

Trust in God, the rest will follow.

He looked toward the marble statue, offering a silent prayer. Standing, he exited the pew. He had to believe Ginger would survive the night. The moment she woke, he'd tell her how very much he needed her.

If she'd have him.

And right now it was a great big "if."

Vince returned to the bustling hospital corridor. Over the loudspeaker came the words, "Code Blue to ICU. Code Blue to ICU."

Fear slammed into him like a freight train traveling at maximum speed.

His heart raced, and his head pounded as the realization hit him.

Ginger was in Intensive Care.

Running down the hallway as fast as his legs would take him, Vince headed in the direction of her hospital room. Tearing around a corner, he narrowly missed colliding with two wheelchairs and a patient strolling leisurely down the hall with an I.V. stand at his side.

As if in the clutches of a nightmare, Vince's legs seemed as heavy as cement. The faster he tried to go, the slower his limbs moved. Finally reaching the ICU, he took a deep breath and closed his eyes. He wanted to slide to the floor and weep like a baby.

It wasn't Ginger who needed life-saving medical attention. He pitied the sufferer in the other room who did, but was infinitely grateful that Ginger, at least for now, was managing to get by with the help of the many machines connected to her immobile body.

Through the glass walls, he watched Ginger lying defenseless on the stark white hospital bed. Her friend, Robyn, sat in a chair by her side, talking to Ginger even though she couldn't answer back.

"How's she doing?" Detective Miller walked over to Vince's side and nodded toward Ginger.

Turning, Vince leaned his back against the glass. "No change." An hour ago, he would have hated saying that. Now, after the scare of the Code Blue over the intercom, "no change" sounded like a gift from above. Life could be snatched from a body in one fading heartbeat.

"Renard Duchaine confessed the women had nothing to do with the theft at your office," Miller confided. "We've still got him on attempted murder. If Ms. Thompson doesn't make it, Duchaine will be in the slammer for life. There were too many witnesses."

The cold hand of dread traced a finger up Vince's spine. "She'll make it," he announced through tight lips.

"Of course she will. I'm just saying 'if.' " The detective slapped a hand on Vince's back, then walked down the hall.

Needing to touch her, to verify that Ginger was still breathing, still alive, Vince walked toward the doorway to her room.

A petite nurse stepped in his path. "I'm sorry, we're taking her down for tests. You can't go in right now." Despite her small stature, Vince could tell she was a force to reckon with. And right now he didn't have the energy. He was drained. Admitting defeat, he threw a longing glance toward Ginger, turned and went in search of the waiting room and a cup of black coffee.

Sipping the bitter vending machine brew, Vince sank down on the gaudy turquoise plastic sofa in the lounge. He allowed his eyes to close as his head lolled back against the hard cushions. Tiredness slowly permeated his bones like a fog rolling into the shore. He'd just shut his eyes for a minute. No more than that.

His breathing deepened.

Images appeared in his mind. A woman, far off in the distance, beckoned to him. She stood on the edge of a cliff, her blond hair and white dress billowing in the gentle breeze. Was it Ginger? Wanting to be sure, Vince stepped closer. The woman held out a hand beckoning him forward, a look of gentle yearning on her face.

It *was* Ginger. Vince smiled. She smiled back, love shining in her blue eyes. Ginger was alive and she welcomed him. She wanted him in her life. Vince longed to run to her, but his legs wouldn't move. Puzzled, he looked at his feet. Two hands coming out of the earth clung to his ankles in a death grip.

An evil blackness obscured the sun. The wind whipped around them, keeping them apart. Vince held a hand out to Ginger, urging her to come to him. From nowhere, Renard Duchaine appeared at her side. Even though it was dark, the gun in his hand glinted menacingly.

Vince wanted to save Ginger, to tell her to run. He couldn't talk. As if his body had turned into a statue, he couldn't move, couldn't gesture, couldn't anything. He had to stand there and watch in paralyzed fear as Duchaine lifted his weapon, pointed it at Ginger and without any show of remorse, pulled the trigger.

Vince snapped out of his dream, sloshing cold coffee on his wrist. "Damn," he muttered, shaking his head to clear it of the nightmare.

"I'm sorry, I didn't mean to wake you."

Vince's head shot up. Across from him on the other turquoise sofa, sat a fair-haired woman. "Ginger?" The woman looked incredibly like her, but was older. Strands of silver streaked through her hair. The vague hint of wrinkles appeared at the corners of her eyes and around her lips.

"No. I'm Ginger's mother."

"How is she?" Fear clutched at his heart. Reliving today's horror in a dream had scared him. The future scared him.

"She's still down for tests. We'll know more in a little while."

Vince pushed back the heavy hair covering his forehead. An oppressive weight filled his stomach. How could this woman sit in the same room with him and not want to kill him for what he'd done? "Ms. Thompson. You must despise me."

The woman's head tilted to one side in a manner that imitated Ginger and his heart lurched. "You're right. I should hate you."

Vince sucked in a deep breath. He'd expected this, but was surprised at how much her words deepened the pain in his chest.

"I don't, though. I never realized how

much time I've wasted until I saw my daughter lying in the hospital bed." The woman's eyes filled with tears. She looked across the room at Vince, her hands twisted together in her lap as if the memories were almost more than she could bear.

Confusion washed over him. "Why are you telling me this?" he asked.

She spoke so soft, Vince had to lean forward to catch her words. "I don't want my daughter to suffer the pain and loneliness I forced myself to endure. I'm asking for your forgiveness."

What was she talking about? "Forgive you? What for? This is all my fault." Had he missed part of a conversation somewhere? He stared at the ceiling rather than look into the eyes that so resembled Ginger's.

The older woman stood and moved to Vince's side. Sitting next to him, she patted his hand in a friendly, soothing manner. "The only person to blame is the man who pulled the trigger. You had no way of knowing any of this was going to happen. Nobody did."

Vince turned his head and looked deep into Eva's eyes, past the sympathy and understanding, past the pain. He tried to delve into her soul — into her true feelings. If it was his daughter . . . hell, he didn't know what he'd do. He struggled with his words. "That bullet was meant for *me*."

"Maybe. Maybe not." She shrugged her delicate shoulders.

Vince shot her a look of disbelief. Why was she trying to twist the truth? "He was my enemy," he said shoving a thumb into his own chest. "Ginger had never even met him before."

"Oh, I'm not denying the man wanted to harm you. It's just the Lord works in mysterious ways. Things might not have turned out the way he intended if you had been shot instead."

It was the second time in a matter of hours the presence of God had been shoved in front of his face. He wasn't sure he was ready to handle it. "What are you talking about?" Again, he was missing a piece of the puzzle. "What would have turned out different? I don't understand."

"If you had been shot instead, would you have realized you loved my daughter?"

Vince squeezed his eyes shut, then quickly opened them when the memory of holding Ginger's bloody body slammed into his head. *He loved Ginger more than he'd ever loved anyone in his life.* "I wish it had been me instead of her."

"Of course you do. You love Ginger. You wouldn't be here if you didn't. Ginger loves you, too."

The hammering of his heart pounded in his ears. Ginger loved him? "She told you that?"

Again, Eva tilted her head. The hint of a smile played about her lips. "Not in so many words. You have to understand, my little girl and I have a complete understanding of one another. We may not always agree, but we know what the other is thinking. Sometimes we communicate without speaking. Last Christmas she said there was someone very special she wanted me to meet. That man never materialized. Ginger moped around for weeks like a lovesick puppy." Reaching out, she squeezed Vince's hand. "Am I right in assuming you were that man?"

With tears forming in his eyes and a lump in his throat, Vince could only nod.

"I'm sorry to say this now, but at the time I was glad. I didn't want her to get hurt. What a fool I've been," she sighed. "The absence of you in her life has hurt Ginger far more than your presence ever could have. I don't know what happened between the two of you, but let me tell you from my experience, don't let pride get in the way of love. Your dignity won't keep you warm at night.

The more layers you pile on, the colder you'll get."

Vince thought of his longing for Ginger and the gut-wrenching desire to crawl into the skinny hospital bed and wrap his arms around her forever. "I don't have any pride left," he muttered.

"Good. It's a useless sentiment." Ms. Thompson stood and held out her hand. "Let's go see how my daughter's doing, shall we?"

When Vince stood, Eva tucked his arm around her elbow as if it was the most natural thing in the world for her to do.

Together they pushed through the double doors separating the rest of the hospital from intensive care. Behind the glass windows, swarms of doctors and nurses buzzed around Ginger's bed blocking her body from Vince's view. His stomach clenched and his heart beat a wild tempo against his ribs. Robyn stood outside the door. Tears streamed unheeded down her face.

"Oh, my God." Ms. Thompson tore her arm away from Vince's, her face drained of blood, and ran to Robyn. "What's wrong?"

From behind, Vince put his hands on the older woman's shoulders, ready to help if she fainted. Robyn looked into their eyes and started crying again.

"Has she taken a turn for the worse?" he demanded, grabbing Robyn's arm and giving her a gentle shake.

"No." The beginnings of a smile lit up her face. "She's awake," Robyn beamed. "Ginger's finally awake."

Relief washed over him, its power so intense it almost knocked Vince off his feet. He leaned his forehead against the cool window, the taste of his own tears on his lips.

"The worst is over."

Vince looked up to see a doctor in green scrubs standing in front of Ginger's mother. He walked to Eva's side on wobbly legs.

"We'll keep Ginger in Intensive Care through the night, just to be on the safe side, then move her to the main wing in the morning. You can go in, one at a time for five minutes each. She is still very weak. Whatever you do, don't excite her."

They all watched the doctor walk over to the nurse's station. He picked up a clipboard and began writing notes in rapid strokes.

"You go in first, Vince." Eva gently pushed Vince toward the door.

Fear assaulted him. His hands trembled and he clenched them at his side then shook his head. What could he say to her? How could he possibly begin to make things right between them? "I don't have the right."

"You have every right. Remember what I said about pride? I know in my heart Ginger needs to see you — needs to know you care. Now get in there before I change my mind."

"Okay," he managed through his constricted throat. Vince stepped into the doorway and lifted his gaze to the figure lying on the bed. Blue eyes stared back. A weak, but tremulous smile graced Ginger's face. Vince took a hesitant step forward. Under his breath he thanked the one being he'd never believed existed until now. "I owe you one, God."

With nervous apprehension, Ginger watched Vince sink into the chair at her side. The hand reaching for hers felt cold and clammy. Was that really Vince standing there or just a dream?

"How do you feel?" he whispered, his green eyes searching every inch of her face.

She didn't have the strength to lift her head off the pillow. But having Vince sit next to her with what looked like love shining in his eyes was a heady experience. "I feel wonderful," she rasped through dry lips.

Bending down, he kissed her forehead with infinite tenderness.

"Vince," Ginger whispered.

"What?" He grabbed her hand between both of his and held it to his lips.

"Can you ever forgive me?"

A shadow crossed in front of his eyes.

Fear blazed through Ginger's body and her bottom lip trembled. He couldn't. And why should he? She had been nothing but trouble for him since day one. Nothing but a liar.

"We can't talk about that now, Ginger. You're not strong enough. The doctor said —"

"I don't care what the doctor said. I need to know now. Do you forgive me for lying to you when we first met?" Tears slid down her face and dampened her pillow. He didn't love her. He probably just felt guilty because she stepped in the way of a bullet meant for him.

"Calm down, sweetheart. I loved you from your very first lie. Besides, there's nothing to forgive. At least not from you." Vince scooted his chair even closer and all but climbed into the bed next to her. "The question is, can you ever forgive me?"

Of course she could. "For what?" Had he said he loved her?

"For doubting you. For not trusting you. For not proposing the first night I met you."

Despite her weakened state, Ginger's heart thumped wildly in her chest. "Propose?" Propose what? That they'd never see each other again? That they'd forget they ever met?

"Propose," he flashed her a devilish grin that made her insides quiver in a way she knew had nothing to do with the medicine the doctors had pumped into her.

"Propose?" she asked again.

Vince traced the outline of her lips with one finger. "Hurry up and get well. I think a Christmas wedding would be beautiful, don't you?"

Ginger's eyelids grew heavy. "Boy," she whispered. "These are great drugs they've given me. I'm hallucinating." She giggled. "I'm dreaming that *you* want to marry *me*. Isn't that a kick in the pants?"

"Only if you don't feel the same way."

Ginger tried to open her eyes. Through the tiny slivered opening, her image of Vince was fuzzy and distorted. "I wanted to marry you the first time you kissed me. But everyone knows you don't always get what you want." A weak laugh escaped her lips before she began to fade out completely. "Next thing you know you'll be telling me you want to go skiing on our honeymoon."

Chapter 13

A chill wind whipped Ginger's hair around her face. The scent of pine trees tickled her nose and with one mittened hand she wiped a dusting of snowflakes off her lashes.

Adjusting her goggles, Ginger took a deep breath, pushed off the top of the hill and began her descent. She had to admit to herself that she was getting better at this skiing stuff. But just when her confidence was rising, a child darted around her sending a spray of crystalline snow into her face.

Ginger, her balance lost, teetered precariously to one side, then toppled over. She lay on the cold ground staring at the cloudy sky when a man skied into her vision and stood above her.

"Don't just stand there," she said, holding out a hand. "Help me up."

The man in the black ski outfit unfastened his skis from his boots. Impaling the pointed ends into the snow so they wouldn't slide away, he took her skis out of their bindings, then grabbed her hand and pulled

Ginger up and into his arms. "Mrs. Danelli," he drawled, a sexy smile playing about his lips. "How can a woman so unco-ordinated on the slopes be so . . . coordi-nated in the bedroom?" He raised one black eyebrow in question.

"I don't know, Mr. Danelli," Ginger pouted as she tried to rub her body sugges-tively against him. When she lost her bal-ance, she grabbed the front of her husband's jacket to keep from falling.

Vince laughed and pulled her closer. With one gloved hand snug around her waist and one cupping her chin he bent his head. His soft lips touched hers in a searing kiss that heated up even her cold feet and threatened to melt the snow beneath her into a puddle.

"Mmmmm," she murmured. "Tell me why, Mr. Danelli, we are out here on this freezing slope when we have one very warm, very big bed awaiting us in the Honeymoon Suite?"

"Good question. Last one there is a rotten egg." In one quick motion Vince released her, snapped on his skis and raced down the hill.

Hurrying, Ginger put her skis on. "Whoah!" The skis finally gave in and slid out from under her. With a whoosh she landed on her butt. "Men," she mumbled, trying to get up gracefully. "Can't ski with them. Can't ski without them."

Finally making it down the hill, Ginger checked her equipment and headed up the elevator to their hotel suite. Sliding her key card into the lock, she opened the door to the sight of a hundred candles twinkling in the darkened room. A seductive trail of white and red rose buds led the way into the bedroom.

Ginger followed them, rounding the corner to the bedroom. Vince lay on the bed propped up against a mass of pillows. He was covered with a white silk sheet from the waist down except for one tantalizing leg. That one, sexy, muscular leg was propped up with his arm resting on top.

Ginger's mouth watered at the sight of him. He was so handsome. So devastatingly sexy. So very much hers.

His green eyes twinkled. "What took you so long?" he asked in a seductive whisper.

Ginger decided not to tell him that she had stopped at the gift shop on her way in. To tantalize him, she slowly unzipped her red parka. Watching his face, Ginger let the garment fall seductively off her shoulders, then to the floor. She knew the exact second he realized she was wearing a flesh-colored teddy underneath.

Letting a smile play about her mouth, Ginger unzipped her pants and let them slide to the floor with the jacket.

"Honey, if you don't get over here in about two seconds, I'm going to have to come after you."

Running across the room, Ginger flew over the edge of the bed and landed on top of him. He grabbed her around the waist and changed their positions, pressing himself on top of her. "Do you know what you're doing to me, lady?"

"Of course I do," she whispered, trailing a finger down the fine hairs on his chest. "Don't you trust me?"

"With my life, baby. With my life."

About the Author

Amy Sandrin has written stories since she was a little girl. She never considered herself an author, though. Writing was just something she did, another facet of who she was. The writing went in hibernation while Amy concentrated on college, then marriage and a baby. Years later she took up writing again, and whether she wanted to label it or not, the title of author took hold and stuck fast. Not only does Amy pen award-winning fiction novels, as an avid quilter she's also published bestselling, nonfiction quilt books. She lives in the Pacific Northwest, outside of Seattle.

The employees of Thorndike Press hope you have enjoyed this Large Print book. All our Thorndike and Wheeler Large Print titles are designed for easy reading, and all our books are made to last. Other Thorndike Press Large Print books are available at your library, through selected bookstores, or directly from us.

For information about titles, please call:

(800) 223-1244

or visit our Web site at:

www.gale.com/thorndike
www.gale.com/wheeler

To share your comments, please write:

Publisher
Thorndike Press
295 Kennedy Memorial Drive
Waterville, ME 04901